# WITHIN THE SHADOWS

KINSLEY KINCAID

Written by - Kinsley Kincaid

Cover Design by – Kinsley Kincaid

ASIN – B0BMZXM1SQ

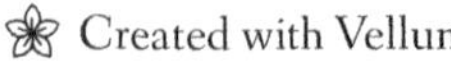
Created with Vellum

*May they all kneel before you and worship you as the filthy Queens you are.*

# NOTE FROM AUTHOR

Please be aware this book contains many **dark themes** and subjects that may be uncomfortable/unsuitable for some readers. This book contains **heavy themes** throughout. Please keep this in mind when entering Carter & Emerson's story. Content warnings are listed on authors social pages.

This book and its contents are entirely a work of fiction. Any resemblance or similarities to names, characters, organizations, places, events, incidents, or real people are entirely coincidental or used fictitiously.

If you find any genuine errors, please reach out to the author directly to correct it. Thank you.

# ONE
# CARTER

Fuck. Even the filthiest porn doesn't do it for me anymore. I stop jerking my semi-hard cock, blowing out a sigh as I tuck myself back into my boxers. I used to love watching this shit. I would edge myself until the very end, not letting my orgasm hit until it was time. The feeling of finally being able to cum was fucking incredible, like a reward after holding it in for so long. Now, fuck. It's been nine months since I've gotten off. Just one day, it stopped.

I know what you're all thinking, 'Carter, why don't you just do hookups or swipe right for the night?' I've done it. It gets old fast. Night after night. Go out, find the girl, impress the girl, bring her home, fuck her brains out and send her on her way. Sure, it was great, but I need something more now. My thirty-four-year-old brain is craving a more genuine connection.

Sitting at the edge of my bed, letting my body fall back to hit the mattress, I stare up at the ceiling. It's 2 am now. Since I can't sleep or jerk off, here's a little about me.

I am an IT guy. The fucking best at what I do. My home base is Chicago, also home of deep-dish pizza and the Bears. I've been doing contract work since I dropped out of MIT. The curriculum was boring. I already knew everything they were trying to teach; coding since the age of thirteen does that. I was strictly there for the piece of paper that would help me land a job; without that paper, the odds of getting any IT gig were slim. So, to MIT I went. Computer Science was my major, but by the second semester, I couldn't do it anymore. I was more intelligent than most of the professors on staff. Fucking, morons.

After I dropped out, my parents were pissed off and, in their words, 'disappointed in my life choices.' I was determined to show them I could fucking do it without a fucking piece of paper saying I had the credentials. Knowing I wasn't going to get a job based on a resume, I went straight to the dark web and started taking contracts. It's not as scary as it sounds. For the right amount of money and a semi-ethical contract, then I am at your service. You must vet these contracts meticulously to ensure they aren't FBI or other international agencies trying to catch you doing something illegal. If you don't, the next thing you know, they are kicking your parents' front door down and arresting you.

The first contract I took was at nineteen, and the rest is history. I primarily hack systems for the highest and most reputable bidder. I am my own boss and do what I want when I want.

Plus, most contracts are offered to me these days

because they have heard of my skills and my ability to keep my mouth shut.

I have a reputation and credibility amongst the world's most powerful and, at times, illegal beings. They only know me by my handle, SADMAN23. I am careful that nothing traces back to me and my true identity.

Ok, enough about me. That shit is boring.

Grabbing my phone, I start scrolling through my Snapgram. My profile has no pictures, and I don't follow anyone. I am simply User8392765382. As I mindlessly scroll, this one post catches my eye. You can't see her face, but shit, that body is sexy and those curves. I bite my fist. She is wearing a black lace bra and matching panties, a pink leather-like harness that crosses over and around her full breasts and goes around her stomach and those 'manhandle me' hips, and then the pink leather branches down to her thick thighs like a garter on both legs. She is kneeling on wood flooring, her one hand squeezing her left breast while her other hand is holding the phone to take the picture. The caption reads, '*Freedom feels like this. Thank you*'

Fuck, who is this girl?

Getting up and walking over to my computer, I input her username @tatorsntemptation and let my program work its magic. I built this program myself. I can put minimal information into it, and it finds everything I need. After a couple of minutes, we have a hit. My program continues to run on one monitor while information starts to appear on another.

Emerson Parker, nineteen years old, from Woodsland, Oregon. She's fucking gorgeous. Long wavy brown hair with these dark chocolate brown eyes. Her lips are plump, with the Cupid's bow defined. Her driver's license information comes up next, telling me she is five foot one, with a DOB of June 26 and a perfect 150 pounds. Now for the dirty details of her personal life. She has no siblings, both parents are dead, shit. She is a high school graduate, works at a small diner in town and never went to college. A picture of a cabin pops up next. This must be where she lives. It is a small one-bedroom cabin outside of town, with a tiny porch off her front door. It looks like that is all the information on her. It's not a lot, but just enough for me. I lean back in my chair, pull out my phone again and find her page. My dick instantly gets hard. This is the first time in months I have felt this way. My dick is officially running the show now. I need to see this girl. I need to know more about her. With a heavy sigh, I say out loud to no one other than myself, "looks like I'm going to Oregon."

# TWO
# EMERSON

"Order Up, Emerson."

Walking over to the kitchen window and yelling back, "Thank you, Steve," as I grab the hot plate of Steak and Eggs for our regular at the diner, Brad. He is fifty-four and a widow, his wife died nearly ten years ago of Cancer, and he never dated or remarried. It makes me sad. Knowing he is alone and this every evening being his adventure out. Every day he comes in at the same time and orders the same thing, medium steak with sunny-side-up eggs and white toast with butter. He takes his coffee black, no sugar. Sits in the same booth by the window.

Dolly's diner is in Woodsland, Oregon, it's small but comfortable. I graduated high school last year but decided not to go to college. I don't know what I want out of life yet. Right now, this is where I want to be, working here, which is also like my home away from home. It has the same aesthetics as when it first opened in the mid-'90s; red vinyl booths, hardwood stools, and white and black square flooring. We are retro without even trying. I am one of four servers who work here, Heidi, who is sixty-two years old, is another, plus two part-time students who help during the evenings and do the weekend shifts. Heidi usually opened Monday to Friday, and I would work the mid-day to closing shift. We close at 8pm, but I usually stay late to make sure everything is clean and prepped for Heidi.

Heading over to drop off Brad's dinner, I hear the front door open. Looking over, I notice this beautiful, tall man walk in. I have never seen him before. He has to be over six feet, with shaggy black hair hanging a bit over his forehead, beautiful brown eyes, and thick eyebrows. His lips are pressed into a thin line, I'm unable to get a read on him. Taking a seat at the counter, he pulls his phone out while shaking his head, quickly types something and puts it away. He doesn't seem happy with whoever is on the other end. Shit, I'm staring. Leaving Brad, I quickly walk back behind the counter and gather my composure. My cheeks feel warm, am I blushing? This isn't like me. He is just a boy. He is a beautiful boy, I mean man. He is all man.

Emerson, get your shit together. So, taking a few deep breaths, I go in.

"Hello, welcome to Dolly's. What can I get for you?"

He looks at me still with zero expression on his face and with his deep expressionless voice, "Coffee with no sugar, one cream and a menu?" With my eyes wide, I realize I didn't give him a menu before asking. Come on, Emerson, what is wrong with you? He is just a pretty mysterious man.

"Oh, shoot, yes, sorry about that. Let me grab you that coffee, and here is a menu." Smiling, hoping to hide the fact I am a complete mess right now.

Walking over to the drip coffee machine, I grab a white coffee cup, add the cream, pour the freshly brewed coffee, and head back to him to drop it off. As I set it down, he speaks without looking up from the menu, "Cheeseburger, salad with Italian dressing."

"Sure thing, coming right up."

Making my way to the kitchen window, I place the slip on the ledge and call it back to Steve, "Cheeseburger, salad with Italian dressing, please."

"You got it, Emerson."

Yeah, I really wish I did.

# THREE
# CARTER

This has to be the best cheeseburger I have ever had. It's almost 7pm at a middle-of-nowhere diner, so to say I was not expecting much would be an understatement. This Steve guy really knows what he is doing. It has the perfect amount of ketchup and mayo, with lettuce, tomato and cheese on top of this thick juicy patty. Even the bun is soft, like it is homemade. I am so into this burger that I almost forget why I am here. Her. Emerson. My shy, little dove. She keeps glancing my way when she thinks I'm not paying attention. I am always paying attention. It's my job to pay attention.

Feeling my phone buzz in my pants pocket again. I know who it is, and he won't take no for a fucking answer. His name is Marco, I've done jobs for him previously, and he wants me for an upcoming one. I have told him I'm on a break multiple times in the past three days. Thank fuck, I don't need the money, so saying no is pretty easy for me. But Marco is what the world would call a 'bad guy'; he has enemies, and he wants to fuck his enemies. He wants me to help him fuck them. He is Mafia royalty or some shit. I do the job, give them what they ask for and get paid while keeping my nose out of their business. It's really that simple; many guys in the industry get greedy or double-cross their original contract with the other side. They tend to get found body part by body part, or never found, actually. That is not my endgame. I like being alive and prefer to stay that way until I die naturally, much later in life.

When I grab a contract, depending on what it is, I will either go to the general location of the job or head to my safe house in Chicago. I take the mobile setup that I've put together. I never work out of my own home. It's another precaution I take to avoid getting caught, to never be found, and to keep my anonymity. For this trip, I left everything at home. Emerson is my current mission. I have everything I need to know about her on my phone, in the cloud. Always have a backup.

I feel my phone buzz two more times, but ignore it. He can either accept no or wait until I am good and ready to take it.

I take the final bite out of my burger, licking my fingers and then wiping them on the napkin. Then, I finish my coffee; it's decent. I've had better, but this will do for now. I am staying at a shit motel in town, they don't even have coffee machines in the room, so I will take what I can get for now. I place my cup down as Emerson asks, "Are you done with your meal?"

I clear my throat, "Yeah, thank you."

"I hope you enjoyed it. Steve is a great cook, really the best in town. He can make anything taste amazing.

It's like he's some sort of food wizard... Oh, I'm sorry I'm rambling," saying as her cheeks turn a rosy color from blushing.

You can tell she's nervous and it's clear that I'm the one who has made her feel this way.

I fucking love it.

"Yeah, it was good, thanks." Not making eye contact and coming off generally annoyed and uninterested, so she doesn't realize why I'm really here.

For her.

She stays standing in front of me, holding the plate a moment longer, you can tell she is embarrassed for over-sharing about Steve. Finally, shaking herself out of it, she walks away.

Oh, Emerson, you are a shy one, aren't you?

I look around the diner. The only other customer is getting up to leave. He leaves a couple bills on his table as he puts his jacket on. Just as Emerson walks out of the back as he's leaving, "Bye, Brad, see you tomorrow. Drive safe!"

"Thank you, Emerson, great meal as always. Be safe getting home."

"Thanks, Brad, I will."

Yeah, Brad, she will. I will make fucking sure of it.

## FOUR
## CARTER

I have long since finished my meal and left the diner, sitting in my rental car in their parking lot. The sun has gone down, and it's cold as fuck out. I check my phone, and it is 9:55 pm. Before I came here, I hacked into the street camera system to watch when she would leave each night; it was always 10pm on the dot. Only a few more minutes to wait now. It pisses me off, she shouldn't be working alone this late. But I know her only friend is her coworker, Heidi, who typically opens after Emerson's closing shift. Em likes to make sure things are set up for Heidi; her heart is good and pure, unlike mine. It's nothing to her to take care of others, but who is taking care of her?

Me. That is my job now.

Lost in my thoughts, I almost miss her leaving the diner and walking to her car. It's an old beater Volkswagen that is rusted to shit, and as she turns the engine on, you hear it squeak like it could go at any moment.

That shit doesn't fly with me. She will be getting a new, more reliable ride.

I see her put on the seat belt and drive out of the parking lot onto the main road, heading out of town toward her cabin in the woods. I give her a few seconds head start before I turn my vehicle on and follow her. I need to keep my distance, so she doesn't suspect someone is following her. I don't want to scare her.

Yet.

I follow her ten miles down the main road, which turns into the highway once you leave Woodsland. It's pitch black except for the moonlight and our vehicle headlights. The dark, thick Oregon forest is on either side of the road. You can't see but a couple feet into the tree line. She puts her right blinker on and turns onto the gravel road, which travels through the thick forest that surrounds her cabin. I pull over to the side of the road to give it a few minutes before I follow. She will get suspicious if she sees my car, headlights on or not, since she is the only cabin down this road. After a few minutes, I turn my headlights off, slowly drive the car forward, making the same right turn she did. I don't see any signs of her tail lights, which means she should already be parked and inside her house. Her place is off to the left of the gravel road, only a couple miles in.

I decide to park my car and turn it off just before the left-hand turn to her place. Unbuckling my seatbelt, I quickly open my car door and get out, hoping she doesn't see my car's interior lights before closing the door gently. I make my way up her driveway, using the thick treeline to keep myself hidden. It's even colder out here than it was waiting outside the diner for her in my car. You can see your breath every time you exhale, and I'm thankful I decided to wear a thick black hoodie today.

As I walk closer to her cabin, I slowly maneuver between the trees and dodge branches. Her front room light is on, and I can see perfectly inside through her window. It looks like she has already changed out of her diner uniform into a thin long black t-shirt and black shorts with fuzzy pink socks on, her gorgeous brown hair still in the ponytail. My dick twitches at the sight of her.

Grabbing my phone out of my pants pocket, I open the camera app and make sure the flash is off. I will not get caught and be known as the creepy guy who takes photos of hot chicks in the woods. I snap a few pictures of her warming up food in the microwave. She must have brought it home from the diner. I snap a couple more when she moves to the couch in her living room and turns on the tv. Her place is perfect for her. The kitchen and living room are within the same small space, with a room off the main living area which must lead to her bedroom. She has a gray couch and a dark wood coffee table, which she currently has her feet on as she rests her plate of food on her legs while she eats.

---

A FEW HOURS HAVE PASSED. I'm sure my balls have climbed inside me by now. It's fucking cold out here. But, being able to watch her like this makes it worth it. Finally, she turns off her TV and living room light. I can see the silhouette of her walking to her bedroom, thanks to the natural moonlight shining tonight. She flicks her room light on and closes the door. That's my sign; time to go. I start making my way back through the trees to the rental, which is when I feel another vibration in my pocket.

Fucking Marco.

# FIVE
# EMERSON

It's been three days. Three days since I saw that gorgeous man who came into the diner. I can't stop thinking about him. He was much older than me. I could tell from the lines around his eyes. He also looked so tired. When I looked into his deep brown eyes, there wasn't a spark within them. It was missing, and possibly for some time. I liked that he wasn't jacked like a bodybuilder, but also appreciated that he wasn't too lean. He definitely went to the gym. He didn't smile or talk much. I wonder what he would look like smiling.

Suddenly, I hear the door open from a customer walking into the diner. It breaks the spell of my daydream, and I head over to the counter where the customer sits.

Jimmy is a regular, and he's here for his pickup order.

"Hey Jimmy, how's it going?"

"Good Darlin, just picking up dinner on my way home from work. Fall is really starting to settle in. It's crisp out there. You'll wanna make sure you got a jacket."

He mentions as I walk to the kitchen window to grab his to-go box. I put it in a brown paper bag and, while handing it to him, "Will do, Jimmy. Here's your order, and your total is $17.50."

"Here's a Twenty, darlin'. You keep the change, and have a good night." Telling me as he stands up from the stool.

I take the twenty-dollar bill with a smile, "Thank you. Enjoy your dinner and drive safe."

He nods at me as he turns to leave.

It's a quiet Tuesday night at Dolly's, which I take full advantage of. I've started the prep for Heidi's opening shift. She's my best friend, and yes I know, how strange for a nineteen-year-old to be best friends with a sixty-two-year-old, but she just gets me. She understands and embraces my shy awkwardness and encourages me to always branch out and try new things. So, one day I took that advice and made a Snapgram account where I could post photos where I feel completely free and liberated.

I may wear this classy cream button-up top and red skirt with beige nylon's diner uniform; note the sarcasm. But, underneath it, I am rocking the hottest white lace bra and panties. That is what makes me feel good. It's exciting. To be the only one with the knowledge of what I am wearing underneath this grubby outfit.

So, I decided to create a Snapgram account where I take photos wearing what makes me feel confident and free. This way, I can express myself without showing who I am. That girl on my Snapgram is the authentic and raw Emerson.

This girl right here, wearing my Dolly's uniform, is far too shy to show off in my day-to-day life.

The community on the app is incredible. I get so many encouraging comments from other females who appreciate what I post. I am short at five foot one and curves for days from my larger breasts to wider hips and bottom. But I embrace it, and if posting those pictures in sexy underwear and harnesses help others to embrace themselves, then why not.

Catching myself in a smile now just at the thought of it all, I shake my head and continue my morning prep work for Heidi, getting the to-go cups stocked up front, making sure she has enough ground coffee packages and cutlery sets wrapped and ready for her. The only thing I have left for my closing shift is putting the stools on top of the main counter and doing my finishing sweep and mop. I look at the clock, and it's ten minutes until close.

I'm getting out of here before 10 tonight.

---

I DRIVE the ten miles home to my cute one-bedroom and one-bathroom cabin within the beautiful woods of Oregon. I love my home. It's so peaceful and beautiful. Waking up to the birds chirping every morning is so calming. I don't care what anyone else says about the cold and rainy weather or being out here alone; I love it.

I park my sweet elderly Volkswagen car on the gravel driveway and turn off the engine. Grabbing my bag from the passenger seat, get out of the car and lock it.

It's a beautiful evening, taking in the fresh, crisp air

and night sky as I walk to my front door and unlock it. Fall is my favorite season.

I head inside and close the door behind me. At the same time, I drop my bag at my feet and take my black runners off. It feels so good to get those things off. I prefer no shoes whenever I can.

As I head to my room to shower and change, I feel my phone vibrate in my pocket. Pulling it out, I check it and see an unknown number has sent me a text.

*Lock Your Door.*

Um, what the fuck?

I immediately reply,

*Who is this?*

***undelivered***

Walking quickly to the front window, I peek through the window and see no one out there. But a shiver travels through my body. I feel uneasy, so I close the curtains, walk over to the front door and see I did miss locking it. How did they know?

Turning the latch of the deadbolt, I lock my door, at the same time, I feel another vibration in my hand, and the notification says,

*Good girl, little dove.*

# SIX
# EMERSON

Thank God it's my day off. After last night's random texts, it took longer for me to fall asleep. Not because I was scared, but more out of curiosity, like who is watching me? Why are they watching me? How did they get my number? How can they message me, but I can't message back? I had so many questions, and it caused my brain to run rapidly for hours instead of sleeping. The last time I looked at the clock before my eyes closed, it was around 3am; it's now 1pm.

Rubbing my eyes, I blow out a deep breath and roll out of bed. I don't have anything planned for my day off, and as tempting as staying in bed all day sounds, I shouldn't. I grab my phone off my nightstand and don't see any new texts. A part of me is disappointed that I don't have any more messages from whoever that was, and the logical part of me is relieved. I head into the main room, where my kitchen and living room are, and set sight on my coffee machine. I need coffee to function.

I open the top of my drip coffee machine, put in the

coffee filter and start scooping the coffee grounds in, and hit the start button. Within minutes, I can smell the delicious blend of coffee, it's a local blend, and my mouth starts to water. Have I mentioned I love coffee!

Heading over to the cabinet that holds my coffee cups and other dishes, I grab my favorite cup. It is black with a white cat on it which says 'Coffee Meow.' I wait a few more minutes for my coffee to finish brewing and pour it into my cup. Unable to wait another minute, I take the biggest gulp of this fine beverage. I love coffee, hot coffee.

I walk into the living room with my drink, sit on my couch, turn the tv on and grab my laptop. I took a few photos in a new body harness I got the other day. It is white with silver metal accents and has straps going over my shoulders which connect to the white waist belt. I wore it with a white set of bra and panties, it looked so good together.

I don't photoshop the pictures I post on Snapgram, but I do edit them. I like them to have a particular look when it comes to it. If I post them in color or black and white, I want them to look like those classic Marilyn Monroe-style photos from back in the 1950s. Opening the program on my laptop, I play around with a few photos, applying grainy filters to make them seem like older photographs. I crop out my face, keeps me anonymous and allows me more freedom.

---

SOME TIME HAS PASSED when I grab for my coffee cup to take a sip and realize it's empty. Then I look at the time and see it's already past 3pm. I lose track of time when I edit. I get lost in the art and beauty of it, wanting each photograph to be perfect but also tell a story. The main message I want to show in each is to love yourself and be confident regardless of your curves and size. I am short with a larger chest and hips that don't lie, and I want others like me to know you don't need to hide or be ashamed. We are sexy as fuck, ladies.

After saving my photos, I set my laptop down and decide I should probably eat something. Opening my fridge, not finding anything that is screaming out to me, I decide, junk food it is. I grab whatever I can find from the pantry, chips, cookies and some gummy worms. Armed with all the good stuff, I head back to my little nest I have made on my couch. The tv is still in the background, I have no idea what is on, but I commit to it while I snack. After a few minutes, I have decided it's a survival show. They are alone in the wilderness, having to survive with just a few items they brought. I may live in a cabin in the woods that's as close to nature as you will find me. Dibs out, no thank you to that wild experience, but I am hooked.

---

HOURS HAVE PASSED, and the sun has long since set. I did not plan this, but I have accepted this impromptu binge, really the best way to spend a day off. It's between episodes, so I grab my laptop and open my Snapgram profile. I select the 3 photos I want to post, all in the same harness outfit but different poses, one sitting up on my knees and hand on my hips, another where my back is to the camera like I am walking away. The last one is of me leaning on my door frame, one arm above my head resting on the door frame and the other casually next to my body with my legs crossed. I add the caption 'Smile,' a few trendy hashtags, and I hit post.

I'm startled when my phone vibrates. I don't have notifications on for Snapgram, so it has to be a text. Which is strange for me. I don't have many friends or people who text me.

Grabbing my phone, I see it's another message from unknown:

*Come outside.*

What? I think not.

Yelling into the room, "Whoever you are, I am not coming outside!" I hope they hear me.

I feel another vibration.

*Little dove, don't make me ask again.*

Shaking my head, I go to put my phone back down when another message comes in.

*Are those photos you just posted on Snapgram just for me?*

Ah, so the mystery person follows me on Snapgram. That is one of my many questions answered, but now I have 100 more, like how did this person find me? I may be intrigued, but it's also insanely creepy.

Frustrated now, I stand up from the couch and go to open the front door. I keep my phone on me in case another message comes in or I need to call the police.

"Fine, I'm outside. What do you want?" Yelling out, as I stand in my doorway.

Nothing, no response. Maybe the mystery person is just messing with me, and I am just this crazy person who is outside yelling at no one or anything. Mid-thought, I get another vibration in my hand,

Looking down, I see the message,

*Run.*

Looking back up, then down again to make sure I read it right, I get another message,

*I. Said. Run. Little dove.*

# SEVEN
# CARTER

I am a few hundred yards away from her house as I watch her outside, still in her sleep shirt, shorts and socks, looking at the last message I just sent. Will she listen? Will my little dove obey? A few moments pass, and I start to reach for my phone again, anticipating that I will have to send one more text to her when I see her take off. She heads straight into the forest surrounding her cabin, and I smile, starting to make my way in her direction.

Picking up my pace so I don't lose sight of her, the hunt is on. As we make our way through the thick forest, I hear branches snap and the crunch of leaves under her feet telling me which direction she's going.

I love the hunt, oh little dove. You can run, but you cannot hide from me. I will always find you.

The forest is lit by the moon only, and I see her go behind a tree to hide. I make my way over and watch where I step to not make a sound. She must not know how close I am. I can smell her fear and anticipation as I make my way over to her.

This is the kind of shit that I have been missing in my life.

Now directly behind the tree where she is, I hear her breathing. She is trying to control it, but she's nervously taking short, shallow breaths. It's after a few moments of listening to her I finally make myself known.

Slowly coming around the tree trunk to the front of her, I grab her throat with my hand, applying enough pressure to keep her in place. I am wearing a black sweater with the hood hanging over some of my face, so she cannot see what I look like, along with black jeans and black boots. Her eyes go wide, and the pace of her breathing picks up. She is scared. She grabs onto my arm. Little dove, no need to be scared. We are just playing.

Reaching up with my other hand and I take my thumb, rubbing it along her lower lip, really studying her reaction to it. Her breathing has slowed down, and I can see her eyes have moved from where my face is to look down at my thumb, which is still rubbing her plump lower lip. Fuck, she is gorgeous when she's like this. Scared but curious. I wish I knew what she was thinking right now.

That's when I decide to move my head in a bit, holding it still next to hers, and then I move in just a little bit more and lick her with my tongue. I just need a little taste. She's so sweet. Moving my way up from her jawline, licking her cheek all the way up to her forehead. I breathe in her scent once more before moving back, my one hand still on her throat and the other still rubbing her lip. She still doesn't speak and continues to look at me like, her face is wondering, 'what will he do next?' Now, if I told you, it wouldn't be as much fun.

But, what should I do next? Should I see how far I can take it, how far she will let me? Ah, not this time, little dove.

I remove my thumb from against her lips and put it in my mouth. I need another taste of her, sucking her off of my skin, then stepping back to get a good look at her once more with my hand still gripping her soft and beautiful neck. I take her in, from her cute knee-high socks to the bedtime shorts and her sleep t-shirt. You can see her nipples are hard, she must not be wearing a bra. Fuck me.

I wonder, are her nipples hard because she is also turned on by this? It is a bit cold out, but I refuse to believe it's just the weather doing this to her. I wonder, if I were to check her panties, would they be wet? I find her eyes looking at me. I take one more look at her like this. At my complete mercy. It's beautiful. Then, releasing her throat, I step back further and turn away. Deciding then to leave her here, as I walk away into the darkness of the forest surrounding us. Good job, little dove.

This is just the beginning of our fun.

# EIGHT
# EMERSON

What in the hell was that! Who in the hell was that? My brain is trying to catch up to whatever the hell just happened.

He licked my face. Who does that to someone and then just leaves them in the woods alone?

Then again, who listens to a random text on her phone from a mystery phone number?

I did.

This is not how I pictured my night ending. I couldn't get a good look at his face, he wore the hood from his hoodie, but his hands were big and strong. His breath was minty, like he had chewing gum or mint before licking my face. I think I liked what he did. Licking my face. It felt possessive. Like he was marking ownership.

The thought makes me shiver.

This whole situation is insane. I shake my head to clear my head of all my thoughts. I need a moment to process this. As I take a deep breath in, I shiver from the cold, then realizing I still haven't moved from where everything happened.

Taking my first step on shaky legs from the adrenaline, then another getting my bearings, and I see the light from my cabin in the distance. I start making my way back in a light jog before the mystery man gets a chance to come back and decides to play another game with me.

I think not.

Finally, reaching my house, I open the door and head inside and ensure to lock it.

I stand against the door, letting out the biggest sigh of relief. I made it back, and nothing terrible happened. I'm Ok, everything is Ok.

# NINE
# CARTER

After making sure little dove made it home safe from our quick game, I drove back to the motel where I was staying.

The place is a dive and hasn't been renovated in years, if ever. My room had a queen bed with a red comforter, brown carpet, a bedside table and a dresser which also homed the tv with no cable. The bathroom was your standard toilet, sink and dual tub/shower. The door to the room leads right into the parking lot, which I appreciated. I could come and go as I pleased without anyone noticing me.

When checking in, I paid cash, resulting in no questions being asked. That is just how I liked it. I have been in Woodsland for about a week now. I have spent most of my time watching Emerson from a distance since my first day going into the diner. I am utterly captivated by her. Just thinking of her now in her diner uniform gets my dick hard. I can't explain why I feel this strongly over her or so much so that I want to play hide and seek, but I do.

From the moment I saw her picture, she had me. Yes, her pictures on there are sexy, but it was her confidence that drew me in. It's her empowering energy and not giving a fuck attitude. She is authentic, and she fascinates me. You're probably wondering how I got all that from a few hot photos, right? Well, when you know, you know.

You know what's forced vs. real, and she is real. She embraces her sexy curves and wants to empower others to do the same. You can tell from the comments and replies on her page that she cheers for everyone.

Just thinking about all this, I can feel my dick growing. Fuck it.

I pull up Snapgram finding her most recent post. She is gorgeous. She has a white harness on with a white lace bra and panties. I know I am a massive creep, and she doesn't post to get this sort of reaction out of men, but here we are.

I walk to the bed and lie down, undoing the zipper of my pants and taking my hard cock. I am not one to have a dick-measuring contest, but I was very blessed in this department. Sometimes females from hookups would be intimidated by it. Sometimes they would just kneel before me and worship it. I was 8-9 inches erect. It had been a while since I had seen him in his full form, until her. Now I couldn't get him to ever stand down.

I rub my thumb over the tip, feeling the precum and excitement take over. Then, I wrap my fingers around my cock and start jerking it slowly. I like the buildup.

Looking back at her pictures, I start thinking about everything I want to do to her. Those tits would look incredible with my cock between them, fucking them until I came all over her chest. Scrolling to the next photo of her, with her back towards the camera. That ass, it's like nothing else compares. I will claim that ass. It is mine and only mine. I will prep her for my massive cock with plugs until she is able to keep the largest size in her for an entire day. Only then will I take her.

I quicken the pace of my hand, jerking my dick and scrolling to the last photo she posted, fuck I want that pussy. I need that pussy. It's the only pussy that my dick gets hard for.

She is mine.

I start to feel the tingle in the lower of my back as my orgasm hits me. Cum starts shooting out of my cock, dripping on my hand and the hoodie that I am still wearing. I start to grunt in satisfaction, fuck I never want this feeling to end. I keep pumping my cock through my orgasm. My abs contract as I continue to work myself through it. Pumping myself back and forth. As my orgasm starts to subside, still slowly pumping my cock, I start rubbing the release into my skin and regain control of my breathing.

At the same time, my phone starts vibrating. I grab it off my chest and see it's Marco.

That fucker has the best fucking timing. I am not sure what part of I am not taking the job he doesn't understand, but he is Mafia. Deciding I have ignored him enough, and the fact that I like being very much alive, I answer the phone with my cock still hanging out of my pants. "What, Marco?" I huff into the phone.

"Well, aren't we in a chipper mood, Sadman. I have a job I need you for. You're the only one who could pull it off."

I know he isn't just buttering me up. I am the only one who can ever help him. The job is back home in Chicago. I would have to be there for it, and I have no interest in taking it and leaving Emerson just yet. Our fun has only just started.

"I know, Marco, but I'm not taking any jobs right now. Sorry, my man." With a touch of fake sympathy in my tone.

"I don't think you understand how serious I am. I am not asking."

Fuck, here we go.

"I need you for this job. You will come and help me with it, do you understand?" He demands.

"You are a massive pain in my ass, you know that, Marco?"

He laughs into the phone like this is hilarious to him when I am being deadly serious. He is, in fact, a massive pain in my ass.

"Fine, give me a few days. I will then make myself available. What is the job? How long are we talking here?"

"The job needs to be executed at the end of next month, so if I give you this week to do whatever the fuck it is you are doing, you would have only a couple weeks to prepare and get it done once you get here. Also, I would like to meet you."

"Send the details of the job and targets to my account, so I can see what we are getting into here. And no, you will not meet me, you will never see me, you know the deal. I do my job, I get paid for my job, I leave the job. We never meet." He knows this. I tell him every time he calls.

"You are a stubborn prick, but I respect that. Fine, the details will be sent, and you will be where you need to be within the week! Reach out once you are ready."

He hangs up on me in true Marco style.

Shit. Time to move up my timeline here in Woodsland.

# TEN
# CARTER

It's the next day.

Little dove is working her usual shift today after having her day off. I sit in my rental car, watching her work through the windows. Her shift has ended, and she is doing the last bit of stocking for Heidi's shift tomorrow. She has a soft spot for that woman. Always helps with prep for her morning shift. I checked she doesn't get paid for the extra time she spends each evening doing this. She is selfless, with a pure heart. Opposite of my dark one, it has to be a part of the pull she has over me.

I rub my hand over my face, tilting my head back on the seat. Sitting here gives me a lot of time to think. Self-doubt washes over me. What if she rejects me? She can't. She won't. I won't allow it. She is mine. I shake my head as if it will shake the moment of doubt out of my head. This has to work. This will work.

Lowering my head back down, I notice her shutting off the diner lights, walking through the front door, and locking it. She heads over to her car, shit, I really need to look at getting her a new one. This thing could die at any moment. She needs something safe and reliable. I notice her headlights turn on, and she pulls out of the parking lot. I wait a few moments to follow, as I have done every night since I arrived in Woodsland.

---

AFTER MAKING my way out of town to her cabin, I park out of sight, again. I am not ready for her to see me just yet. But soon.

Once, I see she has made it inside, thanks to the light now coming from her front window. I get out of the car and walk through the forest separating us and stand within the tree line. At first, I don't see her. A few minutes pass, and she comes out of her room, changed into a long white sleep t-shirt that barely covers her delicious ass and her knee-high gray knitted socks. Her hair is in a messy high ponytail, fuck me, I need her. I want to wrap my hand around that ponytail while she is choking on my cock, shit. Unable to wait any longer, I grab a small rock from the ground, and decide to throw it at her window.

After hearing the rock connect with the window, it catches her attention, she looks around but doesn't seem phased by it. I grab one more and throw it again at the same window. Hearing the clank once more when it connects, she narrows her eyes, walks to the front door, and comes out yelling, "You coward! I know you are out here, leave me the fuck alone or show yourself!"

I love this fire in her.

My little dove is pissed, and it makes her even hotter, if that's possible. I don't move. I don't say a word. She waits another moment before turning around to go in. After she closes her front door, I grab my phone from my pants pocket, I made sure it was set dim before coming tonight. This way, she won't be able to tell where I am if she were to look out her front window. It's time to play, after typing, I hit send.

*RUN.*

Looking up again, I see her grab her phone from her bag and read my text.

She looks back through the window I threw the rock at and gives me the finger with a smile.

Making me chuckle, I like her style. Oh little dove, I am going to punish you for that.

I send another text.

*RUN.*

*Do not test me.*

I watch her read the following message. She then puts the phone down on her coffee table, walks to the front door and opens it. Stepping out, still only in her t-shirt and socks.

She looks around again, trying to pinpoint where I am. I can't see her facial expressions from here, but I picture her scowling at me while trying to see where I am. With her eyes squinting and her cute face scrunched up out of annoyance and frustration. She won't be able to see me, no matter how hard she may be squinting. I am in all black again, still standing within the trees. Another minute passes, and she does it.

She takes off into the woods.

Thankful for the light from the moon in the night sky, it helps me see again tonight. Once I give her a tiny head start, I chase after her. I am faster than her, catching up to her quickly as I hear her panting and stepping on fallen twigs, which I hear cracking beneath her feet. Her shoulders brushing against the long branches. I do my best to keep as quiet as I follow her. Part of the fun is her not knowing where I am and how far behind her I am.

My little dove, I will catch you.

She finally decides to hide around a smaller tree trunk.

She must not have learned from the last time. Silly girl.

I slow my pace, to ensure she still can't hear me approaching. I am wearing a black belt with my black jeans and decide to remove it from around my waist. Making calculated movements, I unbuckle it and slide it carefully through the belt loops to avoid making a sound. I want her to feel safe, like she has hidden from me, and I cannot find her.

Once my belt is removed, I take steady steps towards where I see her standing on the other side of the small tree trunk. She has her back to me, leaning against it. I am now within inches of her, I can smell her anticipation.

I move quickly to wrap my belt around her neck and the narrow tree trunk. Catching her by surprise, all I hear is her gasp. I adjust the strap tight enough so she can't escape, keeping a thumb under the belt as I buckle it to make sure she still can breathe. As I finish buckling it, her hands go up to the part around her neck, frantically trying to get it off.

"Why are you doing this?" She cries out.

I have her right where I want her. I don't reply. Instead, I find the zip tie I brought in my pocket, placing it between my teeth. Then in one quick movement, I reach around and grab both her arms, placing her wrists together and holding them with one hand while the other works to secure her with my zip tie. Now she can't escape.

I start to walk away; the goal is to make her think I am leaving her out here alone and trapped. Making sure when I move to step on a few twigs to give that illusion and trigger even more panic in her.

She screams.

It's working.

Oh, my little dove, no one can hear your screams out here.

I love this game, it's called Mindfuck.

I have only heard about them before, maybe saw it a couple times while watching porn, but to actually do one with someone is exhilarating. It's a rush, I could do anything I wanted with her now. Leaving her here for hours alone, in silence. Or moving around and making noises periodically around her, keeping her on edge. The anticipation of what might come next is half the fun.

She is still screaming, so I decide to wait a while more until she stops.

Once her dramatics have ended, I creep my way back. Positioning myself slightly behind her, in order to come up beside her with no warning. She hasn't heard me yet.

Standing behind her now, vanilla and coconut start filling my nose. I am addicted to her scent.

I move slightly to get a better look at her body from the side. Scanning it from her head to toes, I notice her nipples are hard for me again. I reach out and pinch one between my thumb and forefinger, catching her by surprise. Her body jerks, but she can't go far.

"Who. Are. You?" She whispers.

I don't respond. Not yet, little dove.

I fucking love how her body responds to me. Her hard nipples, her breathing has become heavy, and she has stopped trying to fight me. I am starting to think she may even enjoy this. I get hard at the thought.

Letting go of her nipple, I move closer to her and place my hand between her breasts. I start slowly sliding it down her stomach. She wiggles her body in an effort to shake me off. It won't work. I am not going anywhere.

My hand is still moving slowly down her body, over her long-sleep t-shirt. Once I reach the bottom of her shirt, I take my hand and slide it underneath, feeling her cotton panties.

Inching further under her shirt to where I find the top of her panty line, I rub my thumb over the skin just above them, making her shiver. I notice her breathing has evened out, and that's when I decide to move into her panties. Slowly making my way down to her clit. She's so wet. Her body is responding exactly how I want it to. Taking two fingers, I slowly move them to her entrance and thrust them inside her. She gasps immediately at the intrusion.

I find her g spot and start to work it. Her hips begin to

move, and her breathing picks up. Now bringing my thumb to her clit, I begin to circle it simultaneously. She starts to pant and continues to jerk her hips along with my fingers that are thrusting in and out of her. I still don't speak. I just focus on her perfect curvy body and how it responds to me. She is even biting her lower lip until a beautiful moan slips out, "Oh my god."

I feel my dick pressing against my pants, begging to be taken out. I swear I could cum any moment from this.

"Fuck, that feels so good. Keep going," she says breathlessly.

I still say nothing. I just keep working her pussy while she starts to tremble, soaking my fingers. I can feel her dripping down my hand.

"Ah, yes. Keep going. Please don't stop."

Oh, I won't stop this time. Thinking to myself how much fun I could have with this next time. I wonder how she would handle a little bit of edging?

Her orgasm hits, and I keep thrusting my fingers inside her, letting her enjoy this high. She moans as her body gives into me, cum dripping all over my fingers. She is panting, hard. I could listen to this forever.

My own personal lullaby. Fuck, I need to record the next one.

Still feeling a few aftershocks from her orgasm, I slow my fingers down while she's still trying to catch her breath. Once she has settled, I remove my hand from her panties. Deciding then to bring my fingers to her mouth, and she opens for me. I don't even have to tell her too.

I move my fingers past her swollen lips, and she closes her mouth around them, cleaning herself off of me.

Then, her tongue starts to lap them. She can't get enough of her own release.

All of this immediately makes me cum. I feel it shoot out of my hard dick into my pants. My eyes widened in shock. Fuck, this has never happened before. Just by her touch, sucking my fingers. I will never let her go.

Once I've decided that she has cleaned herself off of me enough, I take my fingers out and brush my thumb along her lips. Her beautifully swollen lips. I cannot wait to see them sucking my dick.

I shake my head out of that fantasy, focusing back on the present. Deciding this is enough of the game tonight. I first place my hand over her mouth, so she knows to stay quiet. Next, I move to the other side of the narrow tree to undo the belt with my other hand. Then, taking a switchblade from my back pocket, I cut the zip tie around her wrists. After everything is undone and removed, I take my hand away from her mouth.

She doesn't move.

She's waiting to see what I will do next. Sorry little dove, but this date is over for now. Backing away slowly from where I am standing, I turn around and start to walk away.

Quickening my pace, I make my way back through the deep woods.

I don't want to reveal myself just yet. Smelling my fingers as I continue to walk away, I can't wait to taste her.

# ELEVEN
# EMERSON

I feel like I am standing in place for hours after what just happened. My brain is trying to catch up and process what just happened. And how I think I liked it. The rush. The thrill. It is like nothing else I have experienced with past partners or even from my toys.

I shake my head in an effort to organize my thoughts. I then look around and see I am alone. I have no idea how long I have even been out here. But this seems to be a common theme with him, he plays his game and then leaves.

Like he is the hunter and I his prey.

Why me, and who is he? I have so many questions and no answers or any idea where to start looking for them.

I take one more deep breath and head back to my cabin.

---

MY SHIFT almost always overlaps with Heidi's. If I were to identify someone as my best friend, she would be it. She just gets me. She encourages me to be myself and screw what people may think. Plus, she is the only one who knows about my secret Snapgram account.

I haven't told her about the mystery man yet. I don't want to worry her, and to be honest, I don't even know how I would explain it all to her. I can barely understand what is going on myself. So, until I know more, I am keeping this one to myself for now.

"Em, have you heard of Hinder? I heard on Google it's all the rage these days, sweetie."

"Heidi, keep your voice down! And no, I have not gone on Hinder. There's no one in this town I want to hook up with. I think it just finds other people within your area? And all the rage? What kind of rabbit hole on Google did you go down, H?" I say with amusement back to her. You never know what you will get with Heidi, and I love that about her.

"Oh honey, just put in a different zip code. See what other options there are in the other towns. Maybe I will sign up and see what I can find. I may be old, but I am not broken. Every girl needs that itch scratched once in a while." She says with the biggest smile and winks at me as we stand near the coffee station, our backs to the customers so they can't hear.

"My word, Heidi, who knew you still had it in you!" I am all about empowerment, no matter your age. If she wants it, she should go and get it.

"Emerson, sweetie, I never lost it," saying with a smile and adding a wink.

She has to be my favorite human.

I look at the clock. It's five minutes after her shift ended. This always happens when our shifts overlap. We get caught up talking while we work and lose track of time. It's slow. We only have two customers right now, so it's ok.

"Heidi, you kill me! But go home. You were off five minutes ago," I say with a giggle.

"Ah, look at that. Be good and call if you need anything. I am just going to be at home on my new Hinder." She says with a straight face as she removes her apron and grabs her bag from under the counter. I just stare at her, unsure if she's telling me the truth or not. I kind of hope she will try it.

"Ok, I won't need anything, but thank you. Have a good night!" I say as she walks to the door and waves her hand in the air as she leaves.

---

I GET HOME at my usual time, pulling up my driveway and turning off my car. I grab my bag from the passenger side seat and get out of my car, locking the door.

Grabbing my house keys from my bag, I unlock my front door, open it and head inside. Once inside, I drop my bag and lock the door. I reach for the light switch at my front entrance and turn it on to light up the room. That's when I see them. All of them. At least 20 or so Polaroid photos... of me? What the fuck.

They are spread out on my coffee table, deliberately placed there for me to see. I step closer to the table to get a better look. None are overly inappropriate. I mean, it's inappropriate to take photos of anyone without them knowing, but none seem to be too bad, mostly of me sitting on the couch or wait! My Snapgram photos. But how they're taken is strange. It's like a Polaroid picture taken of the phone they are on. A picture within a picture.

Clever, I kind of want to try this for my own Snapgram.

No, Emerson, stop. This is creepy as fuck! Get with it. This is not normal. But, this can also only be one person.

Without a second thought, I gather up the photos and walk into my bedroom. Once I reach my bedside table, I open the drawer and place them inside and close it. He will not intimidate me. He will not scare me. I keep telling myself this as I start undressing from my uniform and head into my bathroom to shower. When I turn on the bathroom light, I see it. On the mirror in what looks like my pink lipstick?

*little dove*

It's him. What point is he trying to prove? He has violated my space and did this. What gives him the right?

I scream. Loud. From frustration. This isn't ok. He has crossed the fucking line. My line may not make sense at this point in time, but this is my home. All boundaries have been leaped right over by him.

Walking toward the shower, I turn the taps and wait for the water to heat up. I am still at a loss for words as tears start to pool in my eyes. This is all so overwhelming and confusing. Why is this happening to me?

Jumping in the shower, I wash my body and hair quickly. I can't stop thinking about how he was in here. I just want to clean my mirror off and decompress from these last twenty minutes, process and decide what to do next. Logically, I should call the police. But I don't even know who this person is. How would they be able to find him? I get out of the shower, grab my towel and start to dry my body and hair. Placing the towel back on the rack, I lotion my skin and brush my hair.

Heading back into my room and I put on my white sleep t-shirt and knee-high knit socks. As I leave my room, a strong hand goes over my mouth. My heart drops into my stomach, and my eyes go wide. It's him, it smells like him.

"Don't move, little dove. I'm not going to hurt you. I would never hurt you," whispering in my ear.

His voice is quiet and deep. It's definitely him.

I nod my head, so he knows I understand.

He lets go of my mouth, and I slowly turn around. I feel oddly safe with him, and I know logically I shouldn't. But I do. Hearing his voice in my ear calmed me down a little. I can't explain it, and I don't feel the need to question it right now.

My eyes are looking at the ground. I first notice his shoes, black Timberland boots. Then, making my way up his body, I see he is in tight black jeans and a black hoodie, with his hands in his pockets. I then get to his face. I know this face. I have seen this face. He is the hot guy from the diner! With his shaggy black hair, beautiful brown eyes and those lashes. Strong jaw with a little bit of stubble starting along it.

My eyes go wide. I still have yet to speak. I am in shock. My brain is racing, trying to piece everything together. What does he want with me?

He steps towards me, closing any distance left between us. We make eye contact. Then. Then he grabs my face with his hands, leans in and kisses me. My eyes couldn't get any wider if they tried.

His lips are so soft against mine. He is being gentle, and I don't expect it. I close my eyes and let the kiss take over. Again, logic says this is insane. I ignore logic. I kiss him back. Opening my mouth to deepen the kiss, feeling his tongue brush against mine for the first time, something ignites inside me. I try to take control of it now, feeling my breathing picking up. In that moment, instinct takes over, and I bite his lower lip, pulling it between my teeth. I know I have broken the skin just enough to get a taste of his sweet copper blood on my taste buds. He starts to devour me after that. He must have liked what I just did as much as I did.

His hands move away from my face, and I feel them grip my ass, then picking me up. Is this man insane? Breaking the kiss, I pull my face back. I look at him in shock while wrapping my legs around his hips, "Put me down. Are you insane? You can't carry me!" I am not self-conscious, but I am aware of my size. I am not ashamed, but I also know I am not as light as a feather.

Looking back at me, I see the corner of his mouth rise as he shakes his head. The mystery man doesn't say a word. Instead, he starts walking toward my queen size bed in my room. Once we get to the edge of it, he puts me down gently.

"Take my belt off, little dove."

Without a second thought, I follow his instructions. I reach out, unlatch the buckle to his belt, and slide it out of the loops of his black jeans. Once entirely removed, he grabs both of my wrists with one hand, grabbing the belt with his other from my hand. He starts to loop it around my wrist and pulls it tight, but also ensures one of his fingers can slide under it, not to cut off my circulation. He lets go of the belt briefly to pick me up again and position me in the middle of the bed. Grabbing the long piece of belt remaining, he ties it around and knots it on the metal spoke of my headboard.

"Now, don't move. I will always take care of you, little dove. And I think you might enjoy the next part." Saying with a smirk.

My mystery man removes his black hoodie, nothing but his naked torso underneath. He's built, but not too much. It's perfect. I start to bite my lip as I eye fuck him, moving my gaze down his body. Once I come back to reality, I notice he is now only in his black boxer briefs. My eyes instantly go wide. He is visibly hard, and it's huge. I hear a faint chuckle coming from him, but I am still focusing on his cock, and my mouth starts to water. He then hooks his thumbs under his waistband and pushes his underwear down. As he pulls them down, his cock springs out. Shit, it is perfect. It has to be the biggest I have ever seen in person, it's slightly curved, with precum leaking from his tip and a thick vein running the length of it.

He grips it with his hand and starts to pump it with his hand, moving it up and down the length, rubbing his thumb over the tip a few times before letting it go.

Kneeling on my bed, he positions himself between my legs. I look down at myself, still in my underwear, white t-shirt and socks. I feel very overdressed for what is happening right now. As I think that, he lifts my white shirt. Rolling up my body with both of his hands, as he gets past my breasts, I get an idea of what he will do next, so I open my mouth, knowing he plans to put it in my mouth to act like a gag. I don't know why I know this, but I do, and he smiles at me when placing it in my mouth, and I close around it.

He then places his hands on my breasts, squeezing them and circling my hard, sensitive nipples with his thumb. They are well over a handful each, it doesn't seem to bother him.

He then starts moving his head towards my right breast, he puts my nipple in his mouth and sucks. Using his tongue to play with it, it feels so good. His soft tongue brushing over my hard nipple, it sends a shiver down my spine. I let a moan escape me.

He leans back, smiling while looking at my body before him. Placing both of his hands on my stomach, they are soft. Then he begins moving them slowly down my body, all the way to my black lace panties. His thumbs go under each side of my panty hem by my pussy. He teases me by rubbing the area with his thumbs, with the rest of his hands gripping my thighs tightly.

I hope it leaves a mark. Having his handprint on me for days to remind me of this night. He then slowly moves his hands to pull my panties down my legs, like he is taking me in for the first time. He doesn't speak a word. Just focusing on me with his hooded eyes. Once my panties are removed, he throws them to the floor, leaving me in only my knee-high socks.

Leaning down, we make eye contact briefly before he lowers himself further and starts to suck on my clit. One of his hands grips my hip to keep me in place, the other slowly travels back up my body, and he squeezes my breast again. I instantly arch my back. Being restrained by the belt adds an extra element of excitement to this. His tongue laps my swollen clit a few times, making me quiver, as he goes back to sucking me, it feels even more powerful than the toys I use. My lower back starts to tingle as I feel my orgasm coming on. He must know because he starts to suck it even harder. My legs start to shake, and he doesn't stop, knowing what is about to happen. I try to moan through my shirt gag, but it comes out muffled. I'm not sure I can handle much more as he keeps sucking. Then it hits, the most intense orgasm I have ever felt. My legs are trembling, and he keeps sucking my clit through it. I feel my pussy pulse as I cum. I know I am making a mess, but I don't care. He plays with me through it, not stopping until he is satisfied he has gotten every last drop out of my body. As it subsides, I try to catch my breath. He looks up at me, and I notice my cum is all over his chin. It's glistening, and he doesn't wipe it off. Instead, he just smiles at me and whispers with his deep voice, “My favorite flavor.”

Then grabbing both my legs, he spreads them further apart and props them up so they are bent at the knee. I am still feeling too weak and shaky from what just happened, and they fall inward, unable to hold them up myself.

"You are doing so fucking good. Now keep your legs spread and knees bent for me."

He lifts them, propping them back up and wide, then he slaps my pussy. I wince at the shock and sting of it. But it feels good. He does it once more, "One for each leg you let fall over just now. Keep them like this, or I will have to punish you again. Only good girls get to cum," he taunts.

Nodding my head, so he knows I understand, I see him grab his cock. His massive cock. Fuck, what I would do to lick it, to suck it.

Jerking it a few times before lining it up with my entrance, he teases me with the tip circling it around the lips of my pussy. I raise my hips a little to communicate to him that I need it now. He smiles at me, and at the same time, he pushes it hard inside of me. I instantly moan through the shirt gag, and it feels like my eyes are rolling in the back of my head. I feel my pussy stretching around him. It fits me perfectly.

He then starts to pull out, just to pound back into me. He grabs my hips to take more control. I let him have it. I give entirely into him. He deserves it for how he just ate my pussy.

"You're taking me so well. You love my big cock inside of you, don't you? Stretching your pussy. Shit, you're being so fucking good for me."

He quickens the pace, panting, and I hear him moaning. Then, he hits the spot inside of me that makes my legs tremble instantly.

"That's my little dove. Giving into me. Such a good fucking girl, aren't you? Should I let you cum?" Saying in the sexiest growling voice I have ever heard.

He keeps slamming into me, hitting the spot as I feel another orgasm coming on. Lifting one of my legs now over his shoulder to get deeper inside of me. I feel my pussy grip his dick like a vice. Never wanting to lose this feeling of him inside of me. Thrusting in and out of me a few more times, he then demands, "Cum for me. Cum now."

That does it. My legs are shaking so much I can't stop it. I don't want to stop it. I hear muffled moans and realize they are coming from me. This is what an out-of-body experience has to feel like. I feel the tingling sensation I love so much. With a final hard thrust from him, I cum. It feels more intense than when he sucked my clit. I scream through my shirt gag in pure ecstasy.

This feeling is my drug. My release is coating his dick as he continues to fuck me. He quickens the pace, and his breathing gets heavy and louder grunts start to leave his mouth.

"Fuck, little dove, this is better than I imagined. Mine. You. Are. All. Mine. Fuck. Your pussy is so tight." His head falls back, and I feel his cock jerking inside of me as his warm seed shoots out of his dick.

"Milk my cock. Take it all. You fucking own me," growling again.

He keeps working himself until every last drop is left in me. Then, after a few more thrusts, he falls forward.

He lays on top of me with all his weight and his cock still inside me. He then moves his arms up to wrap them around me. To hold me while he catches his breath as well.

Tilting his head a little, he kisses my under-boob area, then places his head back on my stomach. If my hands were free, I would love to play with his hair right now, to even just rake my fingers through it while we calm down.

A few more minutes like this pass, not a word spoken before he lets me go and leans back. His dick slides out of me, but then he takes his fingers and pushes our cum back inside of me as it starts to leak out.

Then moving off the bed, he removes my rolled-up t-shirt from my mouth and kisses me, whispering into my mouth, "Such a good girl for me."

I like when he tells me I'm a good girl. I feel proud.

Finally, he unties the belt from my headboard and unclamps the buckle to free my wrists. He grabs one in each hand and rubs the area where the belt was. There are red marks and a slight imprint from the belt. But I smile at the idea of it. I like that I can still feel it after it's off.

"Stay here. I'll be right back," nodding my head, unable to speak, he walks away. A minute later, he comes back into the room with a damp cloth and cleans me. Once done, he leaves the room to put it back in the bathroom. I am still lying here when he comes back again, lifts the covers, and crawls under them. Again, I still can't speak. I think I am in shock from the entire experience and still feeling the side effects of the best sex I have ever had. But, as I have done this whole time, I let it happen.

"Come on, get under the covers. I don't want you to get cold."

I climb under the covers to join him, who is still nude and a stranger, in my bed. He lays on his back and grabs me to tuck me under his arm, so I snuggle into him and rest my head on his chest.

I am too tired to think of how insane this still is. As my eyes start to get heavy, I give into the sleep. The last thing I feel is him kissing the top of my head before I am completely out.

# TWELVE
# CARTER

The morning light wakes me, the morning sun shining through her bedroom window. Opening my eyes, I see she's still in the same position, her head on my chest, sleeping peacefully. My little dove did so well last night.

I was worried. I had never done anything like this before. This is completely out of character for me from the beginning, but something about this confident, sexy and delicious little dove, my little dove, has brought out a side of me I didn't even know I had. I have only seen these things in the porn I watched. I also know I am not the most ethical person, but I have never stalked someone I found on the internet like this before, and I certainly have never played these games with another female. It all felt so good, so right, though.

Deciding I need to get up, I slowly start to move my arm out from under her so as not to wake her. Then I adjust my body to slide her head from me to the pillow.

After completing this maneuver, I wait another minute before I get out of bed to make sure all this movement doesn't wake her. She needs her sleep. Last night was a lot for her, both of us, really. So after making sure she is still asleep, I get up, walk to the other side of the bed, locate my underwear and jeans, throw them on and head into her kitchen.

Coffee, I need coffee.

I rummage through her kitchen, finding the coffee grounds and fill up her coffee pot. As I wait for it to brew, I locate a cup, and the sweet smell of coffee fills the room. Once it finishes, I pour myself a cup and take a sip. I like it hot. I turn around to lean against the counter and take another sip. As I lower the mug from my mouth, I see Emerson standing in her bedroom doorway. I can't read her face. Is she mad? Is she ok? Has she called the police on me? Fuck, I really hope she hasn't, but I wouldn't blame her if she did. This entire situation is new to me too, she brings this out in me, and I feel alive again.

"Who are you?" She asks in a quiet but confident voice. Her eyes slightly squinting, like she's trying to figure me out.

I don't respond. I just look at her, taking her in.

She's so beautiful in the morning. Messy hair, sleepy eyes and those pouty lips.

"Answer me. Who. Are. You?" Repeating herself.

I shake my head, looking down, then back up at her, "Carter."

I have never told a random person my name before, that shit I keep on lockdown. I don't need anyone finding me or knowing what I do. But yet I tell her, without a second thought.

"What do you want from me?"

"You." I say with absolute certainty.

She shakes her head at me, "You don't even know me. How could you want me? How did you find me? You're not from around here. I don't recognize you at all."

I don't respond right away. This next part is going to really piss her off. I need to word it just right.

I rub my face with my free hand, then go for it, "Snapgram."

"Snapgram? You found me on Snapgram? And thought, what, I'm going to go find her. I'm going to basically stalk her, send her cryptic texts, break into her house and fuck her?" She responds with absolute annoyance, which I can't blame her for having. Fuck, she is so cute like this.

"Well, when you say it like that, I sound like a fucking psychopath. But yeah, Snapgram." I'm slightly embarrassed at how juvenile this sounds, but it's the truth.

"No, no, because you did do all of that. You are a psychopath. I don't post what I do to have the male population think that's an open invitation to find me and treat me like this. I can't fucking believe it. I post those pictures to empower other females and because I fucking like taking the pictures."

Shit. Shit. Shit. She's pissed.

"Little dove, no, it's not like that, I swear. Your photos and what you do for the community are incredible. You are fucking gorgeous, and I am obsessed with your curves, with your confidence. But, as soon as I scrolled past one of your posts, everything stopped. I could feel my heart beating in my chest. I have never felt this way before. I had to find you. I had to... I had to have you. You are mine. My little dove from that moment. I have never acted this way before, and I don't fully understand what has come over me, either. But please, try to understand."

She cuts me off and stares at me like I have grown horns or something, "Do you hear yourself right now?"

"I know. I... I'm sorry. How I have gone about this... it is a lot. I know. I don't fully get it myself, Emerson."

She looks at me. Like really looks at me, like she is seeing into my soul to see if what I am saying is true. I feel slightly uncomfortable, being the vulnerable one for once, and I don't like it. The silence seems like it lasts forever until she speaks again.

"Ok, fine... fine, I believe you. I still think it's completely fucked up. But I believe you, for some reason."

I thank the Gods she does.

"You haven't called the police, have you?"

"No, but I should. This is completely insane," rolling her eyes and shaking her head.

She starts to walk in my direction and makes her way over to the coffee, grabbing herself a cup. Then turns around and stands beside me in silence as we drink our coffees like this is a completely normal situation.

Then. To ruin an already awkward fucking moment, I feel my phone vibrate in my pocket.

I don't even need to check who it is. I know it's Marco. I know he's telling me I have three days left to get my ass back.

Fuck.

# THIRTEEN
# EMERSON

After we drank our coffee in silence, he placed his mug in the sink and went to the bedroom to grab the rest of his stuff.

Coming out of the bedroom, he walks over to me and kisses the top of my head, whispering, "Later," into my hair and leaves. He just leaves.

I wasn't ready to talk anyway. I am still very much angry about how he went about things. It's completely inappropriate and disgusting.

But the sex. The sex was the best I had ever had.

He seems genuine, but aren't all psychopaths good at being genuine? They manipulate us into thinking we are the crazy ones? It's how they think they trick us silly, naive girls. I may be nineteen, but I'm not silly or naive. He has another thing coming to him if he thinks that.

---

I'M ALMOST home from my shift at the diner, where Heidi filled me in on her Hinder antics before leaving.

She did it. She made a profile. She has been swiping right. She's who I want to be when I'm older. I admire her. I'll never tell her that, she will hold that over me, and she doesn't need a bigger ego.

Pulling into my driveway, I notice the front porch light is on, which I did not leave on before I left today. He must be here.

Getting out of my car, I walk to my front door, and that's when I see it. A note taped to the door with one word on it.

*RUN.*

Catching myself smiling. Maybe I'm a psychopath, too.

I drop my bag and start to run around my cabin towards the back.

That's when I feel him.

---

Carter

Standing at the back of her cabin, I see her run past me, and that's when I go. I quickly catch her and immediately use one arm to reach around and grab her around the waist and the other to place my hand over her mouth. Whispering in her ear, "Good job, little dove. I want you to turn around and get on your knees when I let you go. Nod if you understand." She does.

Once I let go, she does exactly what I ask. Fuck. This is going to be fun.

I look down at her, "Now reach up and pull my sweats down. Then take my dick out and suck."

She hesitates, "Little dove, don't make me ask again. Bad girls don't get to cum."

Reaching up to the waistband of my sweats, her hands grip them and start pulling them down past my knees and to my ankles. I decided to not wear any underwear for what I had planned for this evening.

My cock springs out and is already rock hard. It's always ready for her.

Gripping it, I position it in front of her mouth, precum already leaking from it. I rub the tip along her plump lips and growl, "Suck."

Opening her mouth, she moves forward and wraps her lips around it. Taking it deeper and deeper until I feel the back of her throat, "Such a good fucking girl. Taking my cock so well, little dove."

That's when she gags on it, "Just relax your throat and take it. Take it all."

Getting into a rhythm, she works my cock with her perfect mouth, and as I watch her with hooded eyes, I get even harder. I am not small, and she's taking me so well. I see her saliva dripping down her chin and mascara running down her cheeks, thanks to the light the moon gives off.

She wraps her small hands around the base to get

better control and squeezes it. I let a groan leave my mouth. She knows exactly how I like it.

As she continues to suck me so eloquently, I feel my orgasm start to build. She teases me with her tongue moving over the tip. That's when I decide to pull out before I explode in her mouth, "You did so good. But not yet, little dove. I need you to stand up and face the wall of the cabin. Can you do that for me? Can you be my good fucking girl?"

She does exactly as I instruct. Emerson is a fucking goddess. I swear she is bringing me back to life.

Positioning behind her, I lift her sexy diner skirt up to her waist and rip a hole in her nylon's while instructing her, "Brace yourself on the wall."

I slide her panties to the side, she arches her back, sticking out her perfectly round ass. Unable to wait any longer, I bring my thumb to her clit and start to circle it. Then, positioning my cock to her entrance, I slam myself inside her without any hesitation.

This is heaven.

"You take me so well. Such a tight little pussy made just for me, isn't it?"

A moan escapes her mouth, "Yes, daddy, only for you." Fuck, hearing her say that escalates my need for her even more. I keep playing with her clit and pounding into her perfect pussy. It's holding onto me like a vice.

"Do you like this? What I do to you? How your body responds to me?"

Crying out again, I hear her say, "Yes."

"Yes, what little dove?" Needing to hear her say it again.

"Yes, daddy. Your cock makes me feel so good. Harder, please.... Please, daddy, harder."

When she begs for more, that does it.

I jerk my hips harder and faster. Grabbing around her neck with one hand and I continue to brace myself against the wall with the other. I try to get as deep as I can inside her, while having her completely at my mercy. Finally, I feel her pussy clench my cock, and then her orgasm hits, drenching it while screaming my name, "Carter, never fucking stop." Immediately I follow. I cum so hard it shoots in her pussy, and I swear I see stars. Yet, I don't pull out. I claim her as mine each time I cum inside her.

Staying inside of her and removing my hand from around her throat, I rest my forehead on her back to catch my breath.

"You did so good little dove. So. Fucking. Good." I praise her. And I wholeheartedly mean it. She took me so well.

She doesn't say anything, but wiggles her ass against me.

"Fuck. This ass does things to me. I will claim that hole too, and you will let me, just like the good fucking girl you are." She doesn't object to the thought.

Bringing my head up, I pull out of her and grab my sweats to put them back on. She sorts her sexy little skirt out and adjusts her panties. Our cum has to be spoiling them right now, as it leaks out of her. I have never been this vulnerable with anyone, but with her, it feels right.

# FOURTEEN
# EMERSON

His dick is perfect. It does magical things that I cannot explain. And when I called him daddy, I have never called anyone but my dad! But it felt right. It felt good to say it.

After sorting ourselves, I decided he could come inside. I hear him following. I still am pissed at his approach to getting my attention, but his giant dick and incredible sex seem to be blinding me. I've accepted it. It's just sex, anyways, right?

I decide to shower once we get inside, leaving him in the living room. I need a minute to get my thoughts sorted. Standing under the hot spray, I hear the shower curtain move, then I see him. Fucker. But he is so hot. His tall, lean body is perfect. His deep eyes and dark hair hangs slightly on his forehead. He has large masculine hands that I can't wait to feel around my throat again... then his hard cock. I am sure by now he's noticed me checking him out and possibly drooling. Damn him.

Looking at his face, he's smiling with his perfect

teeth. A smile that actually reaches his eyes. It's the most beautiful thing I have ever seen, and I'm totally busted!

Stepping to close the space between us and reaching for my face, he kisses me.

I feel his hard cock immediately brushing against my stomach.

Deepening the kiss, our tongues brushing against each other and sucking the air out from each other's lungs. My breasts push against his chest like we can't get close enough to each other. This is different. The other times we have been together were frantic and not intimate like now feels. This feels like something beyond, if that's possible. I feel him grip my hair and move it to the side, exposing my neck. He kisses his way down to my collarbone, to my breast. A sharp pain follows, causing me to jump. He bit me!

"What is wrong with you?"

"Little dove, I'm marking you as mine," he says with a mischievous smile.

"You're seriously insane," I say, still in shock.

"You can fight it. But it's the truth, and soon you will see it too. So now, are you going to let me fuck your perfect pussy again, or do I have to keep biting these perfect tits?"

Who am I to turn that down? That would be just rude. So, I hook my leg around his hip, and he pounds into me immediately. My eyes roll to the back of my head. He hits me so deeply. It's on another level. With each thrust, he hits the spot.

"Oh fuck. Keep going," I whimper.

"Use your manners, little dove, or I'll stop."

"Please. Please don't stop, daddy. I need this."

"I promise you, I will never stop. You're being such a good girl. Your pussy takes me so well. I'm able to get so deep inside of you. Oh, fuck." He starts to lose control, pounding into me harder and faster, almost like a frenzy has come over him. I match his rhythm, unable to resist.

As my orgasm hits, I feel his as well. We cum together. I feel his cum release inside of me. This is the third time we have fucked without a condom. My eyes snap open as I process that thought.

I'm not on birth control.

Immediately moving back and breaking our connection, I look up at him, point my finger towards the door, and shout, "OUT. GET OUT!"

He freezes and immediately starts to panic, "What just happened?"

"I said GET OUT!" Yelling at him again.

He looks at me for another moment, waiting for me to give him more. But I can't. Once he leaves the shower. I hear the bathroom door open and close.

I don't even know him. Immediately regret washing over me. How could I be this stupid? My heart feels like it could burst through my chest. So, this has to be what a heart attack feels like, right?

# FIFTEEN
# CARTER

After being kicked out of the shower, I grabbed a towel and left her alone in the bathroom. After drying off and getting dressed, I head to her living room and make myself comfortable on her couch. The image of her pussy taking my cock so well is something I never want out of my head. I wonder if she will let me photograph it next time? Shit, what am I thinking? She is pissed at me, again.

Leaning forward with my hands on my head, I try to think about what happened. We had just finished fucking, and she completely lost it. What the fuck is happening right now? Gripping my hair with my fingers, that's when it hits me. I've fucked her bare each time. From my extensive research of her, I also am very aware she's not on birth control. Shit.

But the thought of filling her with my cum brings my dick back to life. Wow, down, boy. Now is not the time. Little dove is mad.

Should I have asked her first? Maybe? Yeah, most likely, I should have. But I needed to be with her without a barrier. She's the only one I've been with like this. Watching her. Hunting her. Little dove and her daddy. The control and need. It's something about her that brings this out in me. These urges, I won't fight them. It feels too right with her. She is mine, and I'll mark her in every way possible. I will fill her with my cum, and she will carry our babies.

The sound of the bedroom door opening breaks my thought, causing me to look up. She walks out, still pissed. I can feel it and certainly see it on her face. She has the cutest little scowl. Her hair is down and wet. She's in a black sleep shirt this time and black knit socks. Like she's making a statement that this is my funeral, message received, little dove. But the way she fills her shirt, I can't look away. Fuck, she is gorgeous.

I stand, walk over to meet her, and immediately break the silence, "I'm sorry, little dove." I take her face in both of my hands, tilting her head, so we look into each other's eyes.

"Are you, though?" Her eyes are red like she has been crying.

Fuck. I hate that I'm possibly the cause of her hurt. I just need to be honest.

"No. Not one bit. I regret nothing with you."

She fires back at me, "Then why say it, Carter?"

"Because you needed to hear it," I say honestly.

"Don't just say things because you think I need to hear it. Stop playing these games and just be real with me. Honest with me." saying in a whisper. Almost like she feels defeated. I can't blame her. What I have done up to this point has been entirely fucked. From the games

I have been playing with her, to the hunt and not using a condom and then cumming inside her. She should have had a say, but I had to have her this way. Nothing could have stopped me.

Pulling her into a hug, I feel her relax, and then she hugs me back. Thank fuck.

Whispering into her hair, "Little dove, let me take you to bed. Let me tuck you in and wrap you in my arms while you sleep."

"Yeah, ok. But don't think this conversation is over. What if I am pregnant. I don't even know you." I feel her shaking while I'm holding her. She's crying again.

Holding her tighter, I can tell she's about to spiral, and her mind is racing a mile a minute, and I hate that I'm the reason, "Shh, little dove, it will be ok. Let's get you to bed, and we can talk about this later." She nods against my chest.

She's going to hate me even more after she wakes up tomorrow.

We will talk later... after I get back from Chicago.

The less she knows, though, the more protected she is.

## SIXTEEN
# EMERSON

*I'm sorry, I mean it this time.*
*But I'll be keeping an eye on you, little dove.*
*-C*

Are. You. Kidding. Me!

I feel the anger on my face, my face immediately feels warm, like I am about to explode.

After I went off on him last night, we ended up going to sleep. Carter had me wrapped in his protective arms, and it felt amazing. I let the anger go, so I could enjoy the moment. But, I know, logical Emerson still hadn't entered the party yet.

But now she has arrived.

I woke up even more pissed off than I already was.

He left. He left and didn't even say goodbye or warn me. He didn't even mention it!

A note. That's all I got. Is that all he thinks I'm worth?

There's some saying about scorned females, and I am that right now.

He is all, 'Oh Emerson, sorry 'little dove' I'm just going to fuck you bare, fill you with my cum, possibly get you pregnant, then leave.'

No word if he will be back. No contact information. So, in 9 months, how am I supposed to text, 'congrats, you're a dad.' IF he did manage to knock me up. I'm only nineteen!

I can't be a mom. I can't be a mom alone!

Ohh, no, Carter, whatever your last name is, you have messed with the wrong girl!

And he has the audacity to say he's going to watch me. Watch away. I don't care. I am a strong, independent female, and I will do whatever I want when I want. Then it hits me. I rush to the living room, where my laptop is and start my online toy and accessory shopping spree. You want to watch me? Well, Carter, allow me to give you quite the show.

---

IT'S BEEN FOUR DAYS.

I just finished a busy shift at the diner and got my period in the middle of it. The timing wasn't great, but I've never been so happy in my life. Even did a little happy dance in the staff bathroom.

I pull up at my cabin and see a box on my porch. It's here! The supplies I ordered. If he is going to be watching, I may as well give him a show. Make him regret the day he left. I don't condone revenge. I'm usually a peaceful person. But Carter is one person I won't be peaceful towards. This is war, Carter.

Grabbing the box on my way inside, I drop it on my couch and open it. It's full of goodies from new harnesses for my upper body and a cute nude lace bodysuit. It has this gorgeous nude belt to go with it, which makes my waist very defined, accentuating my curves. Then my prop. That I'll put to use later after I take a few photos. My new purple silicone rabbit vibrator. She's perfect!!

Leaving everything on my couch, I head to my room to undress and shower. I'm exhausted and bloated from my period. I just want to sleep right now.

Photo fun will have to wait until my next day off.

# SEVENTEEN
# EMERSON

Six days.

Still nothing. But I don't care. I keep reminding myself that. He left. He doesn't care. Why should I? It still makes me so mad, though!

But today is 'Emerson gets revenge day.'

I couldn't be more excited if I tried.

I'm off from work and ready to go. After I wake up, I have my coffee. Then I do my hair in long loose curls. My makeup is very natural since I don't show my face, but I decided today I may show my lips, so I applied some foundation and a deep red lip to go with my nude lace bodysuit. Giving myself a final look over, I can't stop myself from smiling. With my long, loosely curled brown hair draped over my breasts. My curves are on fire in this outfit. I look fabulous.

My camera and lighting are set up in the living room, where I also have my rabbit vibrator on hand.

I've decided to be holding it in a few photos, sliding it down slowly between my breasts.

My first shots will be me lying on my couch. I set up the camera timer and get in position. I place my hair over my laced breasts. My vibrator in one hand with it, slowly moving down my body. My other hand rested over my hair and left breast. I keep one leg straight and the other bent at the knee, falling onto my straight leg. I feel truly like myself when I am like this. It feels amazing.

The camera starts snapping. I adjust my pose slightly every few shots. I then ditch the vibrator, get a few without, and have both hands moving along my curves.

The camera stops, and I get up to move my light and camera around to take a few more photos around the living room. I decided for the last batch to do an outfit change. I change into a pair of high-waisted black lace panties and put on my new black upper-body harness. The straps go over my shoulders, down over my nipples and connect with the waist strap. Again, moving my hair over both breasts to block any nip slips. The Snapgram doesn't like nudity, so I have to be careful.

I lower myself to the ground and sit up on my knees. Having already set the camera timer, I'm ready for when it starts snapping. Again, moving my hands up and down my body, even a few with me leaning forward, hands on my thighs and arching my back. I turn around for the final few, sit on bended knee and tip my head back, so my hair flows down my back and get a few more shots like that. These are perfect!

The camera stops snapping, and now it's time to change, then go through them and pick my favorites to post. Maybe adjust the filter color on a few and ensure anything above my lips isn't showing on my face. I've never been more excited over my pictures. And not for the reasons you may think. At first, this started out as a big fuck you to Carter, but now I think it's turned into one of my personal favorite shoots I've done. Screw him. These are for me. I won't let him take my power like that ever again.

---

A FEW HOURS HAVE PASSED, and I've picked three of my favorites to post today. The others I love, I'll use later. I picked one from the couch with the vibrator, one facing the camera while on my knees, the other with my back to the camera on my knees. I've decided the couch will stay in color, and the other two will be in a bronzed filter. They look incredible. So classy.

I make my caption, '*If you don't believe in yourself, who will?*' And add a few trending hashtags and hit post. I squeal with excitement as I do.

Then I hear my phone vibrate on the couch next to me.

Picking it up, I see I have a new text from unknown,

*Those for me, little dove?*

You bastard.

I type my reply and hit send,

*No. They are for me!*

***undelivered***

Of course. Once giving my phone the middle finger, I toss it back on the couch.

It vibrates again.

It's him.

*Little dove. Do you need a spanking? That wasn't very nice.*

My eyes go wide. He wasn't kidding. He really is watching. Fuck him.

I look around the room. Did he put cameras in here? That's when it occurs to me. Could he be seeing me through my laptop camera? In a panic, I close my laptop, which I set on my coffee table just in case and scream. I scream when I'm mad or frustrated, and he makes me so mad!

# EIGHTEEN
# CARTER

Ten days.

Ten days too long. I hated leaving her. I hated writing that note. It was to protect her. The people I work with aren't entirely sane. I know I'm one to talk, but I'm a saint compared to some of these people. They kill. They torture. They feed off weakness. If they were to find out who I was. They would find her. They would use her against me to get whatever they wanted. I couldn't take the risk. I have to always keep her safe.

The one thing keeping me going is those pictures she posted a few days ago. I know they are a massive fuck you to me. Look what you left behind. I know, little dove, and I hate myself every minute of every day for it. Trust me when I say that.

I can only hope when I get back, she can forgive me. I will beg and plead at her knees. Do anything she wants if it means she forgives me and I'm hers. She's already mine.

This job should be wrapped up in a day or two. I'm at my safe house with all my equipment. Should they find someone better than me to find me, then I can ditch this place. Key the self-destruct code in my system, which wipes it clean, then blows it the fuck up.

This place is registered under a dead guy's name. I always have backup plans and am always prepared for any scenario. No one will know my true identity.

To all these guys, I'm always and only Sadman23.

Marco had sent me the details of the job the day I left Woodsland.

My job is to hack into the Chicago police system with the program I built myself, I have used it on previous jobs. Its purpose is to find a loophole for me to get into their system. Once I am in, I will locate the local PD stationed around the train yard where Marco's shipment is coming in. His guys need to go in undetected.

While all that is happening, I also am ready to intercept any activity on those police radios around the area. I will also intercept any 911 calls made in the area, using a voice-changing program, so they cannot trace anything back.

Then, once I get word from Marco, I need to disarm the train yards' security system. So I did a drive-by of the train yard in a stolen car to see what security service they were advertising on the chain link fence. Information is power in this; knowing what they use makes my job easier.

Once I am in and put the security footage from a few minutes prior on a loop, I give Marco the Ok to go in and collect his product. I also get into the railways' shitty server to remove the cargo from any manifest. Like it never happened, poof, gone. I then reactivate police radios and security systems. No one will ever know we were there.

It took me three days to find a loophole in the police system. Then I was in and able to work my magic. Getting into the trainyards system took me another few days, including their shipping and receiving records and security. They needed to be altered once Marco's guys picked up the shipment.

These guys get shipments regularly through other means of transport, so why did they need me for this? Good question. I had some spare time and did some digging of my own.

I found out our friend Marco was getting a lot of drugs in. I am talking about millions of dollars worth of cocaine. This is a massive risk for him and his guys. If they get caught, it's life in prison, so he hired the best to help. It all made sense now.

Tonight, we execute the job. I'm not worried. I am set up and ready to go. So he needs to not worry about me and focus on his guys getting in and out.

This should take all of a few hours to complete. Another couple to dismantle my setup, then I'm back to Woodsland.

# NINETEEN
# CARTER

The job was a success, of course. There were a lot of moving parts and pieces to watch out for, but it's done. Marco wired the money to my account the minute his guys got out of the yard. I wasn't worried, but these guys love holding money over your head to make sure the job gets done and done right. I play the game, it makes them happy, and they give me my money.

After packing up my safe house, I was on a flight back to my little dove. Once I landed in Portland, I drove the rest of the way to Woodsland in a rental under a fake name. A different fake than I used for my plane tickets. Can never be too cautious in my line of work.

I know Emerson is working tonight. I am scared shitless of her reaction once she sees me. It's for the best that she isn't home. So I head to the diner first and see her. She can't get too mad at me in public and at her job, right? I have never been so scared shitless in my life, and I just did an incredibly illegal job for the Mafia.

---

PULLING the rental into the diner parking lot, I take a deep breath and run my hands over my face. This is it, time to grovel.

She will want to know everything, and that scares me the most. To be vulnerable like that. I have never had to be with anyone before. So many thoughts are running through my head, making me more anxious. I just need to get this over with, rip the band-aid off and start this process. Emerson Parker is worth it all.

Taking one last deep breath, I get out of the car and head to the diners' front door. This is it. Pulling the door open, I hear the bell attached ring, and that's when she sees me.

## TWENTY
## EMERSON

Carter is here.

He's back.

It's been eleven days, not that I am counting. And this is how he decides to pop back up.

I don't think so. My new motto is 'fuck him.'

"Get out, please." Saying to him with a smile and the friendliest tone I can muster up as he stands at the door. He doesn't move. Of course, he doesn't. Why would he listen to me? He always has to be in control. Why would my feelings matter to him? But I have found my voice, and he will listen.

He starts his way over to the counter I am standing behind and sits on one of the stools.

"I said get out, Carter," again with a smile and still very politely. I am at work, after all. But all he needs to do is look into my eyes to see what I really mean, and how I mean it.

Ignoring me, he finally speaks, "Little dove, I'll take a coffee and a few minutes to talk, please?"

"A coffee, that's the first thing you have to say to me since just leaving me? So, you want me to serve you a coffee and just a few minutes of my time? Is that all I am worth to you? I know my worth, and I deserve a lot more than what you just asked for." I'm absolutely floored. His head tilts down, and he rests it on his hands.

"I am so sorry, little dove. I can explain. But you have to know it was all to keep you safe. I always need you safe." he whispers, not looking at me.

What the hell is he talking about? To keep me safe? I am safe. I live in Woodsland. My best friend is my sixty-two-year-old coworker. I am nineteen with a very limited social life. Who do I need to be protected from? Maybe him, since he has been a predator since the moment we met. Even before then, I had no idea.

"Explain." That is all I say back.

Moments pass before he responds.

"I can't, not here. Can I come over after you're off to talk?" He sounds defeated, and I don't feel bad about it one bit.

"No, no, Carter, you can't. If you can't explain it to me now, I don't ever want to hear it."

He sighs, clearly frustrated. Well, so am I!

"Emerson, I can't explain it here. It's a lot of information if the wrong person hears it. I cannot risk it. Not with you."

He didn't use little dove. He called me Emerson. So he is either serious or trying to manipulate me, but I can't be sure which it is.

"No, tell me now, Cater," demanding answers.

"Fuck, I can't. Just trust me, please." He is pleading

with me now, and you can tell his frustration level is rising because I won't give into him. How pathetic. Grabbing the pitcher of water from next to me. He is frustrated with me? He thinks he can raise his voice at me? I think not.

So, I pour it on him, "Then get out," smiling as I walk away.

He looks at me. His face is deadly serious, and slightly in shock that I poured water on him. Then, not saying another word, he gets up and leaves. I watch him leave the diner and get into his car. I'm sure this isn't the last I will hear from him, but he needs to understand I will not fall for his games anymore. I am taking the power back.

## TWENTY-ONE
# CARTER

After she poured water all over me last night, I decided she needed time to cool down. It went better than I thought. She didn't tell me off or tell me she never wanted to see me again, so there is hope.

I went back to the motel I was at the last time I was in Woodsland and booked my original room again for the foreseeable future. After changing out of my wet clothes, I took a shower and headed to sleep. I was not going to give up. Emerson is my endgame.

---

IT'S THE FOLLOWING DAY, and I am ready for round two. I will never give up; I just need time with her in private to explain. Knowing she's off today, I decide to head to her place, hoping she lets me in. Fuck, she has to let me in. I am halfway there, and my anxiety is taking over. So many thoughts going through my head, self-doubt. What if she never lets me explain. My heart is racing like it is trying to escape my chest.

How else can I get her to see what I did was right. I would never willingly leave her. Considering how this all started, she has to know I would never just leave her. I am obsessed with her. I need her. She runs through my veins. She is my lifeline, always.

I pull up her driveway. This is it. This has to work. Gathering my thoughts, I get out of the car and walk to her door. For the first time ever, I decide to knock. I know. I'm trying here.

I knock a few times, and then I hear it. On the other side of the door, I hear footsteps. Thank fuck. Then she opens the door, and I see her. All of her. She is so sexy first thing in the morning, with her messy hair and perfectly fitted oversize t-shirt. It hugs her perfectly.

Her eyes still look sleepy. Shit, did I wake her up? Great start, Carter!

Neither of us speaks. She just looks at me like what the hell am I doing here.

This is it. Here goes nothing.

"Can I please come in, little dove?" I feel broken saying it.

"Why? So, you can manipulate me and trick me into believing whatever story you may have to tell me?"

"Please. It's not a story. It's the truth. Everything I want to tell you is the truth. Anything you want to know, I will tell you," I plead with her.

Another moment goes by, and she drops a stinger right to the heart, "Don't worry, Carter, I got my period, so I'm not pregnant. You don't have to do this. You can leave. It's Ok. I'm Ok."

Fuck. I am such an asshole. Looking up at the sky, I softly whisper, "That's not why I came back."

Realizing the moment I say it, it's come out all wrong. Of course, I would have come back if I knew she was. Shit. Looking back down at her now, staring into her gorgeous eyes.

"That's not how it sounded in my head. Of course, I would have come back if you were, little dove. I was always going to come back to you, always! You are my reason. Reason for being. Since the moment I saw your Snapgram page, my heart dropped in my chest. I needed you. I felt for you, then. I have never done anything like this with anyone else in my life. How I have acted this entire time is something I am not even familiar with. But what I do know for sure is I need you. I will always need you. And I hope to fuck you need me too."

We just stare at each other, allowing her to digest what I just said because there is so much more I need to say.

Opening the door more, "Fine, you can come in."

Yes! We are in. Now for the hard part. Explaining everything.

Will she even want me after?

I fucking hope so.

# TWENTY-TWO
# EMERSON

Yeah, I let him in. I want to give myself closure on this entire strange situation. I will hear him out and then nicely send him on his way.

Walking over to the couch, I sit down, then look at him with a smile, "Well, you can at least make me a coffee after rudely waking me up."

Two can play this game, Carter, and I am feeling very petty right now.

Without arguing or saying a word, he walks over to my coffee machine and starts making the coffee. Good boy, you best not pour yourself a cup because I have no issue dumping that on you, either. The thought makes me giggle.

The coffee is ready, and he only takes one cup out of the cupboard. Call me impressed. He has clearly learned his lesson from last night.

Walking over, he hands it to me, then sits on the couch next to me, letting out a long sigh, "So, where to start?"

I know it's a rhetorical question, but again I am feeling petty this morning and reply as such, "Preferably from the part where you fucked me without a condom, multiple times, then left me. With a note. No explanation. Oh, and you clearly hacked my computer camera based on your texts to me that one day. How about you start with all of that?"

He smiles. He smiles at me. This cannot be my life. I should have used Hinder with Heidi to show him this is not a game to me. This is insane.

Then, interrupting my thoughts, he speaks, "You're right."

Causing my eyes to go wide. I know I'm right, but to hear him say it still surprises me.

"I know. So, start talking, or you can leave."

Tilting his head back, he blows out a loud breath, like he is trying to calm himself down. He then brings his head back down and looks at me. After he licks his delicious lips... what can't a girl look? He then starts to talk.

"I cannot explain why I handled our initial encounters the way I did. Something came over me that I have never felt before or with any other girl in my life. It's like this urge, this primal urge, came out of me, and I needed to play this game with you. To watch you. To make sure you got home safe every night from your late shifts at work. To texting you to get you to come out and play with me. I let this urge take over my body and mind when it came to you. It felt right. When we fucked, not once did I think what we were doing was wrong or risky. I just wanted to fill you with my cum over and over again. And I think you liked it too. Maybe not at the beginning. But I think you started to crave it like I did."

He pauses, but I don't validate these thoughts. Not now. But he is right. The thrill of it was so exciting. I did start to crave it too.

He continues.

"When I got here, I was on a break from work. I manage my own schedule, I guess you could say. But this one guy who I have worked with in previous jobs reached out and demanded I come back from my break early. He needed me for something he was working on. I truly felt like I didn't have a choice. He gave me a week to get back to the city, and once I saw the details of the job, I knew I would be gone for at least ten days, fourteen max. It was a tight deadline, and it had to be done by a certain time and day. So yes, after I got here, I knew I was always going to have to leave you, little dove. But only for a week or two. I was always going to come back."

He takes a moment, then continues to explain.

"I knew if I told you beforehand that I had to leave, you would have possibly pushed me away. Or asked more questions than I was capable of answering. Saying goodbye in person was never an option. I knew I wouldn't be able to leave that day if I had. The note was the only way, in my mind. Looking back on it now, I should have told you, but I need you to be safe."

"You say you need me safe, want me safe. What does that even mean, Carter? Why wouldn't I be safe?" I snap back at him. This isn't making sense to me.

"I do questionable things for bad people, little dove."

His face changes, he seems worried as he confesses this to me.

"Carter, more. I need more than that," because I do. This isn't making much sense to me yet.

"I help bad people get away with bad things. I'm really good at IT, you could say. The flight here, rental and motel are under fake names. If anyone were to find out who I really am, they would then be able to track you through me. You, in their world, are my weakness. They would use that weakness against me to get what they wanted. I cannot have that. Ever. I need you safe always. I could never risk you."

He stops, letting me digest this bomb. Shit. I never expected this.

If this is true, it kind of makes sense. I stand up and start pacing. My mind starts racing.

"So that's how you found me then. Using your computer or whatever? After seeing my profile on Snapgram?"

"Yes. I know everything from where you were born to how you inherited this cottage from your grandfather when he passed. He basically raised you after your parents died. He raised you to be this fiercely strong individual, who I will do anything in my power to protect and win back."

"Leave him out of this. He has nothing to do with this. How dare you invade my privacy like that. What gives you the right!" I snap back at him.

This is unbelievable, but is it? He did basically stalk me, chased me through the woods, and played his stupid mind games on me. Fuck. I feel so confused.

"I'm sorry, you're right. I don't have that right. I won't bring him up again. That was wrong. I don't want to lose you, little dove. I need you. Please," he sounds defeated.

"I don't even know your last name, Carter. You have told me all this shit, and I still don't know who you are!" Still pacing, still trying to understand what my life has come to.

"Reign. Carter Reign. No middle name. I am from Chicago, and I am thirty-four years old. I lost touch with my parents when I entered into the hacking world. I couldn't let them be in danger. They are incredible people, and I just needed to protect them too. No siblings. No serious relationships, just casual hookups, never at my place, and never using my real name. I have played it safe and used fake identities my entire adult life. Not wanting to risk others because of what I do."

I snap back, "Then why risk mine? I didn't ask for this. I didn't want it, so why mine, Carter?"

"I know how this looks. How it sounds. I am a selfish asshole because of it. The moment I saw you, I had to have you in my life. I needed you to be mine. I will always protect you. Always."

He stops, and I think that's it, but then he says, "Do you know why I call you, little dove?"

I respond in a whisper, "No."

"The dove symbolizes love, devotion, grace, purity and hope. You are that to me. I devote myself to you. You are my little dove. Then, now and always."

My eyes water. Shit. Do not cry, Emerson. Do not let him see you cry. I did not expect that. Turning my back to him in order to try and pull myself together. I do not want him to see that he has affected me like this. He will not win.

"I need time, Carter. I need to think about all of this. I don't have the answers you are wanting right now. I'm sorry," I whisper.

"You don't need to say sorry little dove, never to me. I did this. I am the reason for this. Take all the time you need. I will be at the motel in town until I hear from you, ok?" Saying gently.

Nodding my head, so he can see, I add, "And don't follow me home from work anymore. Or hack into my computer cameras. I need time. Alone."

"I understand," nodding his head.

The wood floor creaks as he stands and walks to the door. I hear the knob of the door turn as he opens it, closing it behind him. The loudest scream leaves my mouth out of pure frustration. I don't care if he can hear it. I need to get out of here. So, then I can think clearly about what the hell I am going to do.

# TWENTY-THREE
# CARTER

It's been three of the longest days of my life. Holed up in this shitty motel when all I wanted was to be with my Emerson. But she needs time. And I have to give that to her. If I don't, I know I will lose her forever.

I already invaded her life like a madman, but love does crazy things.

Shit. Is this love?

I have never felt these emotions toward another person before. The need to be around her. To protect her. To watch her. To help her grow and encourage her to do whatever she wants. Because she deserves the fucking world. Even just the thought of this sends a warm sensation throughout my body. Fuck. This is it. I, Carter Reign, am in love.

She is my end game, after all.

If she decides to tell me to leave, that she doesn't want me. I would respect her decision, it would kill me, but I would go. It cannot come to that, though. I won't accept that. I need her.

Mid thought, I hear something by my motel door. Looking over, I see a folded paper has been pushed under my door.

What the fuck? Getting up, I walk over and grab it. Unfolding it and see it's from her.

*My place.*
*Tonight, 8pm.*
*-Em*

---

I AM a mess pulling up to her cabin. I cannot stop my mind from going in the dark direction of her rejecting me. I won't lose her. She is my life. She has to see that.

Looking at the clock on the dash of the rental, it's 7:59pm. I shake my head, hoping to clear it. Then rake my hands through my hair, letting out a sigh. This has to be ok. This has to work.

I get out of the rental and walk towards her door. She has left the porch light on. This has to be a good sign, right?

She cares enough for me to see where I am going in the dark out here. I reach the door and knock. I decide to continue to take a different approach from previous events and hope she sees it as such. I respect her. I am trying to control my urges, and knocking has to show her that. I hear her footsteps on the other side of the door, then she opens it. She is the most beautiful person I have ever seen. Her long dark hair is down in her natural wave, flowing over her perfect tits, which are covered by a black hoodie. Scanning down her body, she is wearing black boy shorts and her signature knit knee-high socks in black. Am I walking into my own funeral again? She is in all black, oh shit. I really hope this is a mindfuck that she is playing on me this time.

I will fuck her so hard if it is, not because I will be pissed at this little show she is putting on, but because I would be so fucking proud of her. Thinking of it brings a slight smile to my face. I love this woman.

"Come in," saying as she greets me at the door.

So, I do, walking into her living room. She has water out for both of us. Oh man, I am in for it.

"May I sit down?" I ask again out of respect. I don't just want to assume things. I want her to make the decision. To show her she has equal control in this.

She nods her head and takes a seat, and I follow. Sitting adjacent to her. I wait for her to start. This is her show now. She is in complete control.

She takes a sip of water and places the cup back down on the coffee table. You can tell she is gathering her thoughts. You can see the wheels spinning. A few moments of silence pass when she finally speaks.

"I have done a lot of thinking over the past few days. Thank you for giving me the space I have asked for. I am sure it took plenty of willpower on your part, being that you have had free-range over me since you got to Woodsland, a lot of it without my knowledge or consent."

She doesn't raise her voice. She is clear, calm and concise. But I also know she is still very much pissed at me and how I went about this.

"As insanely fucked up as it was with the texting me and telling me to run, I still played along. I take accountability for that. And as much as I hate to admit it, I liked it. It was a thrill, a rush, and it brought out desires I had never felt before. I won't lie. I even started to crave it. When will the next text be? Is he watching me now? Then... then you left. You left after cumming inside of me all those times. Not caring if I would get pregnant or not or even asking if it was something I wanted. You just left. No explanation. No contact information was left if I was pregnant. I am nineteen, Carter. Nowhere near wanting to have a child. And you took that choice away from me. You didn't even ask if it was ok. And I was too consumed to realize it happened until it was too late. I know nothing came of it, but something could have, and you didn't give me that choice, and then you left. I was a mess. I thought I was pregnant and would have no way to get ahold of you. Not to add, how this all began was a complete and utter invasion of privacy. Again, taking my choices away from me. You found me on the internet, then found all my information and basically stalked me. Would message me from unknown numbers telling me to run, and I would. Maybe I am the crazy one for listening. I don't know. But you held all the control again, giving me no say or choices in any of what has happened. I like to think I am a powerful, independent, confident female with the freedom to make my own choices. You... you have made me second guess myself since you left. Maybe I'm not that person. Maybe I am weak...." Her voice cracking towards the end. Fuck. I broke her. And not in the way I wanted to break her, I have emotionally broken her.

I am officially a piece of shit.

Placing my head in my hands, I whisper, "Fuck, little dove. I am so sorry. So. Fucking. Sorry."

How do I make this up to her? How do I explain to her this is nothing I have ever done before and she's not weak. She is the strongest fucking person I know. She makes me a better person.

Looking up at her, she has tears in her eyes. This breaks me. Fuck it. She needs to know everything.

"Emerson, I mean it. I am so fucking sorry. I can't take back what I did. I did it. I let my emotions control me, the urges I didn't fight them. I didn't want to fight them. It felt good being so free and being able to be so free with you. I swear to you on my life, I have never done this before. You are the first."

"Oh great," she whispers.

"I regret some of what I have done, but it would be a lie if I said I regret it all because I don't. I don't regret finding you that night online. I don't regret coming here to see you in person. I don't regret the games we played. I do regret not asking you, and not giving you a choice. I should have worn a condom. The need to be inside of you bare and to fill you with my cum overtook all common sense. Leaving you that morning was the hardest fucking thing I have ever done, but I had to. The work I do, if they discovered who I was, then found you. It would kill me. They would use you against me. To get me to do things, I would have said no too. I did that to protect you and us. Please, you have to believe me. I am so fucking sorry for how everything was handled. I will do better. I need you, little dove." I feel completely defeated and entirely vulnerable with that last line. I have never placed all my cards on the table before, but I will for her.

I will do anything.

"I am addicted to you. I need you. Please," I plead. I am not above begging anymore. I kneel on both knees before her and beg while holding both her hands in mine. And I will do this every second of every day if it means she stays mine.

She closes her eyes, and a single tear falls down her cheek. It takes every bit of willpower not to rise up and lick it off her. Make her feel better.

With her eyes still closed. "Carter, this is so fucked up. I need to understand. I need you to tell me everything. I feel like I don't even know you other than being the hot creepy guy who is obsessed with me and basically my very own stalker. I need the truth," sighing, then opening her eyes.

This is it. I have to tell her everything and hope this pure soul isn't disgusted by the work I do for the people I do it for.

"Ok. Ok, you deserve that," clearing my throat as I am still on my knees before her.

"So, shit. Ok... I am an independent contractor, I guess you can call it. I take jobs from people of my choice. These people aren't good people, little dove."

She just looks at me. Waiting for me to go on, so I do, "You could say I am into cybersecurity? I take jobs off the web. The dark web, specifically. They put up jobs, contracts more specifically for people to bid on. If I feel I could do the job, I take it. I go under the username of

Sadman23, so no one knows my true identity. Some have asked to meet me, but I forbid it. I like my privacy."

She laughs, "You like your privacy? You are something else...."

"I know, I am an asshole. I should have respected yours. I should have done a lot of things differently, but I didn't. I will say sorry for the rest of my life if I have too little dove. I swear it." I feel defeated. But I continue, "This last job, I have worked for him before. Marco. He is the Chicago Mafia. He has my burner phone contact information. He hounded me to do this job for him, and I caved. I didn't need to piss him off and have him find someone else who is better than me to dig into me, then find out I was here with you. He would have really had to search because I am the best. But I couldn't risk it. I could never risk you."

Her eyes are still filled with emotion when I look at her, and she speaks up, "Do not put this on me. You left because you wanted to. This is not on me."

Immediately going back and realizing how it sounded, she was right, "You're right. That was wrong, how I said it and how it came out. Fuck, I'm not good with being so open and vulnerable. I have never had to before. I keep to myself. I don't let people in. I am used to one-night fucks, little dove. No one has ever possessed me as much as you do. I... I left because I had to. I did the job because I had to. I knew I had to leave days before I did. I knew I was running on limited time with you, so I took advantage of it. It was wrong. I was wrong to do that. To leave the note, to just abandon you. I didn't know another way. I thought explaining this all to you would make you hate me. I help bad people do bad things, Emerson. I am not the good guy. But you, you are the greatest fucking thing that has ever entered my life. You bring light into my darkness. You force me to come out of my shell and be this person, this person I didn't even know I was. I love you."

There, it's out. All of it. Everything is in her hands now, and I am terrified.

# TWENTY-FOUR
# EMERSON

I am in shock. I think he can tell by the look on my face. I am unable to speak. Just think about and process everything that he just revealed.

He does bad things to help bad people.

He took advantage of me.

He left me.

I make him a better person.

He loves me.

I don't know how to respond to all of this. My thoughts racing a mile a minute. He completely let his guard down. He opened up, took responsibility and didn't try to run from it. I missed him when he wasn't here. I was pissed at him when he wasn't here. I wanted him when he wasn't here. I think I love him too.

I immediately pull my hands back from his, place my head in them, and start crying. This is too much. My body starts to shake. That's when I feel him. His hands go to either side of my head, "Little dove, look at me. It's going to be ok. Tell me, tell me what you're thinking in that pretty head of yours."

It makes me smile. He is insane but completely adorable. With his shaggy black hair in a mess and those deep brown eyes full of concern.

I lean forward and kiss him, completely catching him off guard. Screw logic. I want him. I crave him just as much as he desires me. I, Emerson Marie Parker, am in love with this man.

I deepen the kiss, our tongues touching. Electricity moving through me, reconfirming what I know. This is right. I break the kiss, moving back just slightly.

"What's your last name again?"

He chuckles, still looking at me, "Reign, Carter Reign. And little dove, it will be your last name too, one day. When you're ready."

He picks me up from where I sit. I wrap my legs around him and just hold onto him.

I feel safe. Even if I shouldn't, I do. I know he would never risk me or hurt me on purpose. He loves me.

"I love you, Carter Reign," whispering into his neck where my head sits on his shoulder.

I feel him breathe like a massive weight has been taken off.

"I was so scared, so scared you would hate me. That I was going to lose you. I need you always, little dove. I will always keep you safe. Always. I love you, Emerson."

He walks to my bedroom and sits on my bed with me still clung to him. I am never letting go of this man.

"If we do this, I need honesty, always. No secrets. If

we do this, we're all in or not at all," whispering into his neck.

"Anything, it's yours, little dove. Anything. I will give it up if you want. I have enough money to support us here if this is what you want. I am all in with you."

"I think.... I think I want to see your side of the world for a bit. Experience more," saying with absolute certainty.

"Shit. Are you sure? It's not like how you may see it on television shows or movies. It's risky. It's stressful. It's hard at times. And these guys don't accept me failing. Ever."

"Yeah, I want to see what you do. You have seen what I do at the diner and on Snapgram. I want to see you now. Wait, do you have a secret lair with all your screens and tech?"

Laughing, "Little dove, your imagination is beautiful. I don't have a secret lair. I do have a safe house where I have my stuff set up. This way, nothing gets linked back to me, ever. I take every precaution. Sometimes I have to go where the job is if it's a more difficult contract. I go under an alias, rent a place under it, and buy new equipment that I dump once I am done with it. No traces left behind."

"Can you take a job somewhere amazing next time? I want to see the world, Carter Reign, and I think you at least owe me that considering..." looking at him, I bat my eyelashes a few times. I am really going to milk this for as long as I can. I won't abuse it, but I will see what I can get away with. I add a cute smile to seal the deal.

He shakes his head, "Let's see the world then. This here can be our home. Our safe place. Where we can be us between it all. How does that sound, little dove? Would you like that?"

"Hmm, yes. I think I would."

# TWENTY-FIVE
## CARTER

Holy Shit. She is mine. Forever. She is mine.

I was terrified. I really did think I had lost her. But she sees me, all of me and accepts it. I will worship her every day of our lives, she is mine, and I am hers. Always.

I close the distance between us and kiss her. Hard. Like it's the first and last time we would ever kiss. She needs to know I will always feel this way about her. She is my oxygen, my light in this dark life I lead.

Breaking the kiss, I lay her on her back and look down at her. She is gorgeous. Her perfect breast, her curves that make me weak and that pussy that I call home. I grab her shorts and pull them down; she isn't wearing any panties. This girl kills me, "Little dove, you are so beautiful and in so much trouble. You seemed to have forgotten your panties."

I get on my knees and bring my lips to brush against her swollen pussy. She is dripping wet already. And it's all for me. I start to suck on her swollen clit, and I hear her whimper. I will never get sick of that sound or her taste.

Still sucking on her clit, I insert two fingers inside her wet pussy and start to work that magic spot inside her. I will make her cum as many times as she lets me tonight.

She starts panting, "Oh, yes, there. Don't stop, Carter. Don't you fucking stop."

I'll never stop. I bite her clit, and it sends her into a frenzy. Her legs wrap around my neck tightly, and I feel her body trembling. I go faster, adding a third finger, and that's when I feel her pussy tighten around them. I suck her clit once more, and she cums hard and fast all over my face.

"Ahh, Carter there, keep going. Yes!"

Don't worry, little dove, I am not going to stop.

Still working her until her orgasm dies down.

She drops her legs from around my neck, I look up at her while she catches her breath. She smiles at me. I lick my lips, loving the taste of her release.

Sitting up, I remove my shirt and take my jeans off. Then, removing my briefs, I reach back into my jeans and pull out a condom.

"See, little dove, I've learned," I say with a chuckle while tearing the package open and rolling it on my hard cock.

She giggles at me. That giggle is music to my ears. Then I notice where her eyes are focused on and joke, "You like what you see? Because he is all yours. You own us."

"Good. And I will take very good care of you both," she says back to me with hooded eyes.

And I am done for. Climbing back on the bed, I grab the bottom of her shirt and pull it over her head. Position myself between her legs, grab her wrists, and place her arms over her head. Holding onto them both so she can't move.

I line myself up at her entrance and slam myself inside of her. It's home.

"You are taking me so good. Such a good fucking girl." I then start to thrust inside of her, slow and hard. I have never made love before, but I think this could be what it feels like. I stop moving for a moment and just look into her eyes, she is mine.

Closing the distance between us because there has been enough of that these past couple weeks to last us a lifetime, I kiss her. Kissing her deep and with every ounce of myself going into it. I start moving again, thrusting my dick in and out of her. This is all about her. She moans in my mouth as we continue to kiss. This feels fucking incredible. I keep going, starting to move faster inside her. I feel her pussy walls clench around my cock, and I know she is almost there. I keep going, hitting the same spot over and over. That is when I feel her cum, her release is coating my cock. I keep working her through her orgasm. Letting go of her wrists, I break our kiss and grab her hips. Positioning her at a different angle and start thrusting into her faster and harder. It starts to feel like she is milking my cock with the aftershocks of her orgasm, and that's when I feel my own orgasm about to hit.

Looking directly in her eyes, I cum. My release shooting out so hard into the condom, even with a condom on, it's still intense. I keep thrusting through it.

Panting, I faintly am able to say, "Fuck, your pussy is magic." Once my orgasm subsides, I keep my cock in her. I lay on her chest, head between her breasts. We are both left breathless.

She breaks the silence, "That was incredible."

"Just wait until I take your other hole," it will absolutely happen.

"I can't wait for you to own all of me," she confesses.

Then, wrapping both my arms around her, I just hold her.

"I love you, little dove, always."

# EPILOGUE

## EMERSON - 4 YEARS LATER

I have dyed my long hair black, and it is slicked back into a high pony while wearing a turquoise Prada shorts suit with Prada wedge sandals and you guessed it, Prada oversized sunglasses.

I walk into the target. My sunglasses have been modified to include a camera feature within the lenses, completely hidden and undetectable.

We are in Dubai for a job. When I said I wanted to see the world, he stayed true to his promise. We have been everywhere, from South America to Japan to Iceland and now here, Dubai. I still post on my Snapgram. I still want to encourage females to embrace themselves, regardless of their shape or size. We are all beautiful and should never feel ashamed or embarrassed.

I still don't show my face, I still love the ability to be anonymous. Carter installed layers of IP on my phone, so when I do post, it would be hard or even impossible to track it. He calls it safety precautions. I don't exactly know what it all means, but I believe him. My safety is something he doesn't take lightly.

We are in Dubai because Carter took this contract to help with a jewelry robbery a few weeks back.

Some of the prep work leads us to find the blueprints to this place. They were dated, and the remodel was not on file anywhere. That's where I come in, sometimes, I get to play too.

It does take some convincing, but sometimes I just bat my long lashes at him and promise the best blow job he has ever gotten, and he gives in.

Anyways, back to the job. Focus Emerson.

These glasses are transmitting everything I see back to Carter at our safe house here. He needs to know the layout in case it has changed, along with the cases used to store these gorgeous jewels and the security system watching over the store. I look around, not to be obvious. A worker approaches me, "Welcome. Is there anything in particular I can assist you with today, ma'am?"

Looking up at him from the case, "Yes, I would love to see that bracelet there, the gold one with the emeralds. It is just what I need for my collection."

"Of course, Ma'am allow me." He pulls it out from the case, wearing white gloves to not leave his prints or oil on it. I lean forward to really look at it, it is absolutely gorgeous.

Taking another minute to look at it, to pretend I am really interested to not cause suspicion, I look back at him, "Yes, can you please put this aside. I will send my husband back to get it. I didn't bring my purse with me, I was just out exploring your wonderful city, and when I saw this from the window, I just had to come in and see it for myself."

"Yes, of course, ma'am. And what name shall we use?"

Oh, this is the best part. Hmm what name shall he get this time, "Roger. His name is Roger Montgomery. Once I get back to our hotel, I will send him. Thank you."

He nods, taking the piece out of the showcase area, and goes into a back room. This gives me the opportunity to scan the room for Carter.

"Great work, little dove, now you see that black box on the wall by where he walked. Can you get a little closer to that?"

I have an earpiece in, I love this. It makes me so giddy. Like I am a real secret agent.

I tip toe as quickly and quietly as possible to the black box and scan it with my glasses.

"Did you get it, babe?" I whisper.

"Thank you, little dove, I think we got it all. Time to get out of there," he says back through the earpiece.

Just then, as I start to make my way to the door, the worker comes back out, "Mrs. Montgomery, it's been a pleasure. I look forward to meeting your husband."

Looking back at him, "Yes, a pleasure. Thank you."

I leave the store, walk around the corner and do a little happy dance. It is such a rush. No wonder Carter does this. It's such an addictive feeling. I love this. I love our life.

I make my way back to where we are staying, it is a quick walk from the store. An apartment in an incredible high rise. I wave at the doorman and wait for the elevator.

The doors open, I insert the key card and click our floor, 17. The ride is quick, and the doors open to our place directly.

Walking in, I see Carter still sitting at his setup. Screens everywhere, at least four. A program running on at least two, another one with the video I just took and the other with whatever coding he is doing. He is a genius, and he is all mine. The thought brings a smile to my face as I remove my sunglasses and walk toward him.

Spinning around in his chair, he sees me, "You did so good. This is perfect."

His arms are out, and I walk right into them.

"Now, little dove, put those sunglasses on the desk," he demands.

I do what he says and look at him with suspicion.

"It's time for you to hold up your end of the deal. On your knees, take daddy's cock out and milk both my balls dry. You need it, little dove, since you are eating for two now." He says with a smile.

"Of course, daddy." I love sucking his dick. The thought of it gets my panties wet.

But he is right. We found out a couple weeks ago. We are pregnant. I knew about his intentions this time. Once I start to show more, we won't take any more jobs and head back to Woodsland. Our home base in the cabin. Where it all started.

I still keep in contact with Heidi. I called her immediately once we found out. She doesn't know all the details of Carter and me, just that he is well off and promised to show me the world. I know she suspects more, but respects our privacy and has never pried. She has, though, had some success on Hinder! She met a nice man her age who she sees as needed, her words, not mine. I know she means for sex. I always bug her about it when we talk. I am also not one to judge if he wasn't in her age range, I mean, look at Carter and I. We met when I was nineteen, and he was thirty-four. Now four years later, he gets more handsome as each day goes by.

I can't wait until we get back to Woodsland for a bit and have our baby.

This is my life, my completely insane life that I wouldn't trade for anything. It is my last thought before getting on my knees and wrapping my lips around his monster cock.

Using my tongue, I taste his precum while circling his tip. This move makes his hips buck, further pushing himself in my mouth.

"Fuck, just like that," he groans.

Oh, I'm just getting started, thinking to myself.

I grip the base of his dick with my hands to take better control. Then I slowly start working my mouth down to his shaft.

My own panties are already soaked... I hope I get to cum after too.

Relaxing my throat, I start to take him deeper. As I hollow my cheeks, I move my mouth back and forth, loving the feeling of having him in my mouth and at my mercy.

"Little dove, you're taking me so well. I can smell you from here. Touch yourself. Finger your wet pussy while you suck my cock," he demands.

Of course, I listen. Good girls get to cum.

Leaving one hand at his base, I move the other down my panties to my wet pussy. Inserting two fingers inside of myself, I find my spot and start thrusting them in and out of myself while my thumb circles my clit. I moan, but it's muffled by his cock.

All of this feels so good.

Hearing me and feeling the vibration of my moan in his dick ignites a reaction out of him, he brings one hand to the back of my head and pushes himself further in my mouth and down my throat, gagging me, but then I relax my throat even more, to take him deeper.

I feel tears running down my cheeks, which has no doubt caused my mascara to also smudge.

My lips touch his pelvis, the red lipstick I'm wearing leaving a mark as I pull slowly back to keep working him.

"Fuck, little dove. You feel so good. Keep playing with yourself. Do not stop until I say."

I look up at him briefly with hooded eyes so he knows I understand and keep working on himself and me.

His hips start to move more frantically, holding my head in place. He's about to cum.

Will he let me swallow it, or will he decorate my face with his release?

I continue to edge myself, I want to cum so badly. I am almost there.

"Now. My little cum slut, cum now", he growls as I feel his release start to coat the back of my throat.

I thrust my fingers a couple more times and join him.

My legs shake while I am still kneeling before him. His cum still shooting out of his cock in my mouth. Both his hands are now in my hair, holding me in place, not to waste a drop.

Fuck. This feels so good. I love being daddy's little cum slut, but most importantly, Carter's, little dove.

Pulling my fingers out of me and then my panties, Carter takes my hand and puts my fingers in his mouth, sucking off my release.

His own orgasm has died down as well, releasing his other hand now from my hair, so I can remove my swollen lips from his cock and lean back.

He finishes licking my release off my fingers and tucks himself back in his pants. As I am about to get up, he cups my face with both hands and looks me in the eyes, "I love you, little dove. Thank you. Thank you for bringing me back to life. For giving me this new life and for giving me the chance to be a father. I will never let you down, never. Or our family. I love you both so much."

The End.

# ACKNOWLEDGMENTS

Fuck me. We did it again!!

Thank you to everyone who has taken a chance on this baby dark romance author. I appreciate the fuck out of you! Your excitement makes me excited!!

A guy friend of mine mentioned a dream... a one day wish... that involved chasing his lady love through a jungle. I wanted to give him his fantasy, Kinsley style. So, I give you *Within the Shadows*! If you loved this story, then let us thank him for sharing his jungle fantasy with me on that one fateful day! Without it, Carter & Emerson may not be here. He was equal parts surprised then excited af when I told him I wrote this primal/daddy vibe/computer tech guy (sadly not as exciting of a tech job as Carter don't worry Mr. FBI) book for him and immediately requested multiple copies of it. If you hated the book - you can blame him as well, let's not limit ourselves - haha.

My Alpha and Beta Queens. I adore you!

*Jessica, Mind.fullyx* - babes. Thank you for everything!! Thank you for being my sounding board! For letting me throw ideas at you, and you just accepting it - or saying hmm... tell me more about what you're thinking here - haha! Just thank you for being you!!

*Sandy, Cheyanne, Ashley and Lakshmi* - Thank you for all your funny and incredible comments throughout the doc. They made my life!! Thank you for helping me with my first big release!! And for a couple of you... your wish was my command. I hope the grand finale BJ was as sloppy and delicious in all its glory as you had requested and hoped!!

*The Tainted ARC Team!!!!* I appreciate you and your support more than you'll ever know. Thank you soooo much for everything. I can't wait to show you what other chaos I have in store. Thank you!!

*Tainted N Taboo Reader Group Crew!!* Thank you for being as twisted as we are and joining us for this ride!! TABOO is Coming!

*K.L Taylor-Lane* - you're my hero. My life goals. I love you! I hope we find our tree house.

*Raeleen* - to popping many more cherries!!

*Isla*.ily.

Until the next one babes!
-Kins

# ABOUT THE AUTHOR

Kinsley Kincaid is a long time fan of psychotic dark book boyfriends. She does not limit it to just Dark Romance but Taboo as well, yes the scandal!

She enjoys pushing boundaries, so don't be surprised when you see this also reflected in her work.

Be sure to stalk her on her socials and reader group shared with Isla Gray; Tainted N Taboo

Made in the USA
Monee, IL
12 May 2023

33574888R00075